Mom took in a deep breath that wasn't quite a sigh. "What Lien *said* was that you were welcome to visit Boston provided you didn't mind pitching in at the Mua Xuan Restaurant. She left her number. It's there by the phone."

She then got up and walked out of the kitchen, leaving me staring at the phone. It was like a movie script: after years of trying to locate her birth family, the heroine tracks them down. Now she stands, phone in hand, her heart pounding like a drum, but she can't make her fingers punch those numbers. Finally, with a supreme effort of will, she does it. A dial tone whirs. Clicks. Now she waits.

One ring, two, three, four—and a clear, bright voice sang, "Mua Xuan Restaurant." I stammered that I was looking for Lien Van Tran. "This is Nancy, her daughter. Can I help you?"

I had a blood-cousin named Nancy! She sounded about my age and friendly, too. I stammered, "Th-this is Mai Houston. From Serena, Iowa. I wrote—"

There was a crash in the background, and someone commenced yelling in what I guessed was Vietnamese.

Also by Maureen Wartski
Published by Fawcett Books:

BELONGING
DARK SILENCE

THE FACE IN MY MIRROR

Maureen Wartski

FAWCETT JUNIPER • NEW YORK

RLI: $\dfrac{\text{VL: } 6 + \text{up}}{\text{IL: } 6 + \text{up}}$

A Fawcett Juniper Book
Published by Ballantine Books
Copyright © 1994 by Maureen Wartski

Library of Congress Catalog Card Number: 94-94394

ISBN 0-449-70443-2

Manufactured in the United States of America

First Edition: December 1994

10 9 8 7 6 5 4 3 2 1

Remembering Berta and Hermann Wartski

Chapter One

"THAT," KAY ANNOUNCED loudly, "was the dumbest movie I ever saw."

"Really, *really* dumb," my younger sister, Liz, agreed.

"Dumb or not," I said, "that flick kept us from having to think about Fain's test."

Mr. Arthur (the Pain) Fain had announced today with lip-smacking glee that he was going to hit us with a test on *Romeo and Juliet* tomorrow. "There is absolutely no use trying to cram at the last moment," he'd almost drooled. "Those of you who have studied faithfully have nothing to worry about. Those who have not are in big trouble."

"If Mom finds out you have a test tomorrow, you're in big trouble anyway." Liz sucked on her braces in a revolting way. "Going to the movies before a big test is a no-no, Mai. She'll ground you for a week."

Liz had overheard me talking about Fain's test on the phone to my best friend, Kay Mallory. She'd heard Kay suggest that since studying wouldn't do us any good, we might as well catch an early movie and had promptly blackmailed me into taking her to the movies, too.

"If you're thinking of snitching on me," I warned, "don't. Besides, you'll be grounded, too."

Kay was looking up and down the street. "My brother is such a pain," she complained. "The only reason Jim got Mom's car is because he *said* he'd pick us up at eight-fifteen. He's probably hanging with his dumb friends and forgot the time."

This was serious. I'd managed to talk my folks into letting us go to the movies on a school night only because I'd given my solemn oath to get home by eight-thirty. "We'd better start walking," I said.

It was only two miles from the center of town to our house, but naturally Liz went orbital. "Walking?" she yelped. "At *night*?"

In June it doesn't get really dark, even at eight-thirty. I told Liz that she could either come with us or stay and wait for Jim Mallory alone. She gave me a dirty look, tossed her head, and stalked off. Kay and I fell into step together, talking about the movie and trying not to think of Fain's test.

Serena was the kind of small town that shuts down after eight, so not many people were around. With Liz marching on ahead of us, we passed the library and Dr. Ambrose's podiatric clinic and had stopped for the lights by Hong's dry cleaners when Liz said, "Listen!"

Strange hissing noises were coming from the back of Hong's, and a male voice growled, "That should do it."

"Someone's back there," Liz said unnecessarily.

"Just some kids sneaking beers," Kay began, but her words trailed off as four guys came around Hong's. Three of them were about our age, but one was older. His reddish hair was cropped close to his scalp, and he wore cutoffs and a black T-shirt that had a skull and crossbones on it. He was carrying what looked like a can in his hand.

"Hey, lookit what we got here," he grated. "Your daddy own this place, sweet-cheeks?"

Then he lunged at me. It all happened so fast that I didn't have time even to think—never mind run—before I was knocked to the ground.

As I hit the pavement, something wet, warm, and sticky erupted in my face. "You frigging gooks," I heard my attacker snarl, "why don't you go back where you belong?"

2

He was interrupted by Liz's screams for help. "We're *out* of here," I heard him say.

Then they were bolting away from me down the street. I sat where I was, my hands and backside smarting, and looked dazedly around for my sister and Kay. Liz was standing nearby and yelling for help, but Kay was running down the street away from us.

"Are you okay, Mai?" Liz shrilled.

Before I could do more than nod, three people came hurrying toward us. They were old Mr. Abramovitch and his dog Pegasus, Nate Bartlett, who owns the shoe repair shop in the square, and Mrs. Costello, the head librarian.

Mrs. Costello reached me first. She moved fast in spite of the fact that she was no spring chicken. She had a voice like the brass section of our school band, strong and loud but inclined to go off-key when she was agitated. It was off-key now. "My Lord," she quavered, "oh, my dear Lord, child, what did they do to you? Hurry, Nate—get the police and call the ambulance."

The horror in her eyes made me look down at myself, and I nearly fainted when I saw that I was covered with red, sticky stuff.. Was it blood? But, no— "It's just paint," I heard myself say.

"Go call the police anyway, Nate," Mrs. Costello directed. "And you, Mai," she added sharply as I started to get up, "stay where you are. You may be hurt more seriously than you think."

There was a little gasp. Kay had come back to stand behind Liz, and her eyes were as big as golf balls. Up till then I'd been too dazed to be really scared. Now I recalled the look on those guys' faces, and my stomach soured. They'd *really* wanted to hurt me.

My teeth began to chatter as Nate Bartlett took off, running hard. Mrs. Costello creaked down on one knee beside me, and Mr. Abramovitch leaned close,

3

asking if I knew who'd attacked me. I shook my head. "I want to get home," I moaned to Kay.

But my normally take-charge friend just stood there, and it was Mrs. Costello who said, "Of course you do, but we must wait for the police."

There was a ruffle of sirens, and a squad car pulled up next to us. A young police officer jumped out, took one look at me, and turned pale. "Paint," Mrs. Costello explained in her deep voice.

"I saw what happened," Kay cut in. Her cheeks were pink, almost as if she'd started to enjoy the excitement. "Those creeps were hiding in back of the dry cleaners so's they could attack us."

"They knocked my sister down and spray-painted her," Liz added.

Your sister?

I could see the young cop's lips move on the words even though he didn't say them out loud. He stared at Liz, then at me, then back at Liz again. Mrs. Costello meanwhile blared, "These are the Houston girls, Mai and Elizabeth. Officer, Mai was assaulted by hooligans. What are you going to do about it?"

"You can't go anywhere anymore without there's some jerk making trouble," Mr. Abramovitch put in. "Even here in Serena, where my wife and I, may she rest in peace, lived all our lives, we're not safe."

The young policeman asked me for a description of my assailants and called it over the radio. Meanwhile, the other policeman, an older man who I'd seen around town, had gone in back of the dry cleaner's. "Look at this, Fred," he called.

All of us followed the young cop around the back of Hong's. "Son of a bitch," Mr. Abramovitch muttered tiredly. "So, now it begins here in Serena, too. Out here in Iowa, hate crimes, yet. Who ever learns?"

Enormous red letters had been spray-painted on the wall. In the slowly dying light I read DEATH TO THE SLOPES and GOOKS, GO BACK TO HO CHI MINH CITY.

"First the Jewish cemetery in Ginville," Mr. Abramovitch continued sadly, "and now here they

4

are picking on the Asians. A bunch of no-goods trashed a Korean restaurant in Clanton last night. Hong is Vietnamese, right, Mai?"

Why was he asking *me*? Everyone was looking at me, so I said I didn't know and stared down at the ground.

"And what are the police doing?" Mrs. Costello demanded. "That's what I want to know."

Stiffly, the young officer said that an APB had been issued for the perpetrators. He turned to me, adding, "I'll need your statement, Miss Houston. If you'll come down to the station, we'll send someone to notify your parents."

"I'll do that," Mrs. Costello said. "It'll be easier if I break the news. Elizabeth, go with your sister." Kay said she'd come, too, but Mrs. Costello shook her head. "No need for that. Your parents will be worried. Nate Bartlett will take you home."

Nobody argued with her, not even the cops. People recognized the voice of authority. Mrs. Costello had been in the library for about a hundred years, and everyone in the crowd, including Mr. Abramovitch, probably, had been commanded by her to Be Silent or Leave the Library.

Serena was such a small town that practically everybody at least recognized everybody else. Apart from the young officer who, it turned out, was new in town, almost everybody else on the SPD knew the Houstons. The older officer introduced himself as Sergeant John Barton and told Liz and me that he'd bought his house from our folks' realty company, Houstons for Homes.

"Used to be that Serena was a real nice place to live," he sighed as we drove down to the station house. "Now, maybe because bad elements are moving into the towns around us, jerks with noodles for brains are picking on anyone who's—well, who looks different."

I felt the same prickly sensation I'd had when Mr. Abramovitch assumed I knew whether or not Mr.

5

Hong was Vietnamese. Then I remembered the disbelief on the young cop's face and the names that creep, my attacker, had called me as he aimed his can of spray paint in my face.

I was suddenly good and mad.

Listen, idiots, I wanted to tell them all, I am *not* different. My name is Mai Jennifer Houston. My folks are Vivian and Leo Houston, and I'm older sister to Liz, thirteen, and David Houston, aka the brat, who is eight. I'm nearly sixteen, a sophomore at Serena High School, member of the school chorus, reporter for the *Serena High Crier*. I'm a not-so-successful member of the swim team and a pretty good left fielder for the girls' softball team.

I'm as American as country-western music, I wanted to yell. I grew up in Serena, Iowa. I belong right here.

Liz was nudging me. "I wonder if the reporters are going to interview you," she hissed in my ear. I told her that what happened in Serena didn't exactly make for headline news. "They interviewed that rabbi guy when they messed up the tombstones at the Jewish cemetery," she argued. "Maybe you'll get your picture in the paper with your hair all cruddied up and everything."

As she babbled on, I overheard the officers in the front seat muttering to each other. They used such low voices that I knew they had to be discussing me. As I strained my ears, I heard the young officer say, "Adopted—sure, I guessed that. I mean, it's obvious, right?"

Liz was saying that she didn't know how I was going to get the paint out of my hair, that maybe I'd have to cut it short. "It's really bogus what they did to you," she added, "but we were lucky. I mean, they could have killed you."

"They could have killed you, too," I pointed out, and Liz looked a little sick and said nothing more for the rest of the ride.

6

Once at the station house, Sergeant John Barton sat me down and took my statement. I was almost finished with it when the station door flew open and a pint-size lady with flaming red hair came careening in.

"Mai," my mom, Vivian Houston, fluted, "baby, what did those beasts *do* to you?"

She ran over to me and mashed me in her arms. "Diana Costello called me to tell me there'd been 'an incident.' We all rushed over—Dad's parking the car." She paused to draw breath. "Those criminals didn't hurt you?"

I shook my head, and Liz said rather pointedly that she'd been there, too, whereupon Mom hugged her, too.

Just then, Dad marched in followed by David. Dad stared at me in horror and my little brother went, "Totally rad! Now she's got red hair like the rest of us."

Liz giggled. The brat smirked. Mom said automatically, "David, be quiet."

Dad strode over to me, checked me out to see if I was okay, then turned to the older policeman. "John, have you caught the men who did this to my daughter? I'd like to have five minutes with them, alone."

My dad, Leo Houston, is over six feet tall and weighs about two hundred and fifty pounds. As mad as he was right now, he looked even bigger. I wished, really wished, that he'd been there with me tonight.

"I'd like to oblige you, Leo," Sergeant Barton said. "I don't blame you for feeling the way you do. But believe me, we'll get the punks."

"I want them punished," Dad fumed. "I want to see them locked up for this."

All *I* wanted to do was leave. Mom understood. She told the policemen I'd had enough, that they could talk to me anytime since they knew where we lived. "We're going home now," she announced.

My family formed a phalanx around me and marched me out of that police station, and I caught sight of all of us in the big mirror by the door. Four naturally redheaded Houstons, freckled and blue-eyed, and me. As David had pointed out, my hair was now a stunning shade of black splotched with crimson. Nothing, though, could change the structure and color of my eyes.

Here was this family of redheads and one definitely Asian girl.

Mom caught me staring at myself and misread the cues. "We'll have you looking gorgeous again before long," she vowed. "Come on, baby. Let's get you home."

Chapter Two

GETTING THE PAINT off my arms and face was no problem, but it took forever to get my hair clean. At one point I got so frustrated that I wanted to hack it all off, but Mom wouldn't hear of it.

Finally, near eleven, my hair was back to being black, and the upstairs bathroom smelled like a turpentine factory. The house was really quiet. David had long before gone to sleep, Dad was watching the news on TV, and Mom had told Liz to use the spare bedroom downstairs so I wouldn't disturb her getting to bed.

"Will you be okay?" Mom asked me. I said, sure. All I had to do was blow-dry my hair and clean up the bathroom. "I don't mean that," Mom said. "You had a terrible experience tonight, and I think we should talk about it."

She was standing close behind me, and in the bathroom mirror I saw that her blue eyes were worried and loving. We'd been so busy washing and rinsing and dabbing with turpentine that I hadn't had time to *think* of what had happened, but now I suddenly felt scared. Supposing, I thought, that guy'd had a gun instead of a can of spray paint—

Hastily, I shoved the thought away. "I'm too tired to talk about anything," I told Mom. "I just want to go to bed."

"Okay, we'll talk later." She started to leave the bathroom and then added, "I just want you to know that when Mrs. Costello called me tonight, I realized how very precious my kids are to me."

9

Mom broke off and reached out and touched my wet hair gently, and then was gone, and now there was only one reflection in the mirror. I stood staring at all of me: five feet seven inches with what my mom loyally calls "big bones," long, black, straight hair and a smooth, olive-tinted, oval face. Brown eyes, hazel-flecked, stared back at me.

Me, Mai Jennifer Houston.

Jennifer for my mom's mother, Gramm Jen, and Mai for my biological mother, Mai Hongvan Duong. Mom had given me that name because, she told me, it made me special.

What it did was make you different.

The thought nudged my mind, then skittered away like a skaterbug on a pond. To get my thoughts off this track, I started to clean the bathroom, scrubbing sink and tub and walls. So, I told myself, big deal, some psycho with a chip on his shoulder had made me the target of his pea-brained hate. I'd been in the wrong place at the wrong time, that was all. I was still who I'd always been.

But you've always been different, Mai. Your birth mother was Vietnamese. The Houstons adopted you.

So what? I argued with myself. I'd known all my life that I was adopted. The folks were really up front about that. I knew from the beginning that I'd been chosen, that I was precious to them. And when Liz came along, and later the brat, our parents made sure that I was the big honcho sister, the big cheese. I was never left out of anything. I never felt unloved or was treated differently from Liz or David.

So how come you used to look at the mirror when you were little, and wish you could have red hair and blue eyes, too? Admit that you wished you looked like your American serviceman father, name, rank, and serial number unknown, and not some strange lady called Mai Hongvan Duong.

"Shut up," I told the voice in my head.

The thoughts made me feel uncomfortable. I finished cleaning the bathroom and climbed into bed.

10

Without Liz around, the room was wonderfully peaceful. I closed my eyes, ready to drift off, but sleep wouldn't come.

I'd gone through the stage, once, of wondering what Mai Hongvan had looked like. It'd been simple curiosity, though, a stage that I outgrew. I wasn't obsessed, like some adopted kids I'd read about, with tracing my roots, and I sure didn't want to meet up with the unknown serviceman who'd left me nothing of him, not even DNA that you could see. I had no interest in people and things that had no part in my life.

Finally I fell asleep, and woke up to trouble. With all that had happened, I had completely forgotten about Fain's test. When I remembered, I panicked and told Mom that I was feeling sick from all the turpentine fumes and wanted to stay home from school.

Big mistake. In my panic over Fain, I'd lost sight of the fact that our dad is a fanatic on education. To him, schooling is gold.

According to Dad, he himself had to walk miles through snow and sleet to get to school, and each time he told the story the miles got longer and the snow got deeper. David was lucky—his bus came earlier so he got to escape most of it—but Liz and I were trapped.

"I can't believe you got Dad started on that school thing," Liz huffed as we trudged to school later. "I'll bet it wasn't turpentine fumes at all—you're just scared of that English test you and Kay were talking about." I told her that if she knew Fain, she'd be scared, too, and she went, "So why didn't you study before this? *I* would have."

Last night Liz had stood by me and acted so human that I'd forgotten how snotty she could be. I told her to grow up, and she sucked her braces in that disgusting way she has.

"I'll bet Kay will tell Mr. Fain that she's too *destroyed* by what happened last night to take the

11

test," she said. "That'll be just like her. Look, there she is, telling everybody what happened."

Kay was standing on the school steps, surrounded by a group of kids. "Are you okay?" she hollered when she saw me.

When I nodded, she rushed over to me and grabbed my arm. "I wanted to call you after I got home, but my mom said I shouldn't bother you. I couldn't sleep all night thinking of what happened," Kay added. "We could have both been killed."

She was my friend, so I didn't point out that since she'd run off as soon as the skinheads had rushed me, she hadn't been in any danger. "Boy, it makes me mad," Kay went on. "I wish those dirtbags were here now so I could spit in their faces."

The kids Kay'd been talking to had drifted over and were listening. It was embarrassing. I tried to hush her, but Kay just talked louder.

"It's a lucky thing there were three of us, Mai, or you could've been hurt worse than you were. This isn't L.A. or New York or even Des Moines, it's *Serena*," she went on indignantly, "the quiet, dinky little small town we've lived in all our lives. Who'd think we'd get mugged by guys who are prejudiced against Asians?"

"Asians are lazy and dumb," said a tall, freckled, bony-faced blond boy who had joined the group around us. "You can't trust them," he went on. "All they know is how to steal white people's jobs."

"That's a lie," I sputtered. "Asian immigrants work hard, that's how they get ahead."

"Where did you read that?" he sneered. "The Ho Chi Minh Times?"

I'd seen him around school, but I didn't know his name. I glared at him, but before I could answer him, Liz spat out, "That's the dumbest thing I ever heard anybody say."

"Me, too," Kay said. She added indignantly, "And anyway, why should those creeps attack *me*? I'm not Asian."

12

The homeroom buzzer went off then, and we scattered, Kay muttering at my side that she'd really told that redneck where to go.

I was still mad at what Freckles had said. "You sure did," I said. "You told him you weren't Asian. That makes it okay for them to push Asians around, right?"

"I didn't mean any such thing, and you know it. I was there for you last night."

Kay had raised her voice again so that the kids behind us could hear how brave she'd been, and I was suddenly tired of her grandstanding. "I suppose you told everybody you risked your life for me," I exclaimed.

Kay stopped dead in her tracks and stared at me. "What's got into you?" she snapped. "You're acting weird this morning, Mai. You're different."

Different.

The word was like a wasp's sting, and I spoke before thinking. "Maybe what's got into me is that you *weren't* there for me last night. You left Liz and me and took off, remember?"

The kids behind us craned their necks. Kay turned bright red. I didn't wait to hear what she would say, but I turned on my heel and left her standing there.

It wasn't till I got to homeroom that the guilt started to creep in.

I hadn't been fair to Kay. Anyone would have been scared last night, anybody would have run. If the situation had been reversed, I'd probably have been spooked, too.

Kay Mallory and I'd known each other forever, and we'd been best friends since our freshman year. And yet I'd taken a cheap shot at her because Freckles had made me so mad.

I felt like a toad, and it didn't help that everybody in my homeroom seemed to know about last night's incident and asked me what had happened and how I felt. Even worse, in my first period social studies class, Ms. Tandy lectured for half an hour on how

13

minorities had been persecuted through the years. Every time she mentioned Asian immigrants, she looked pointedly at me and at Morris Woo, who sits across the room. So did the rest of the class.

English was next. I tried to talk to Kay before the test, but she acted as if I weren't there. Then came the test, and it was the pits. By the end of it, even the smart kids were talking to themselves, while I was so destroyed that I could barely manage to crawl out into the hall to my locker.

Maybe if I hadn't been as glassy-eyed as I was, I'd have realized right away that something was wrong. As it was, I just wondered why a group of kids were milling around my locker and why Brenda Wilkerson, who plays left field on our girls' JV softball team, said, "Uh, Mai, maybe you'd better not come over here right now."

Not go over to my own locker? I blinked stupidly at Brenda and then at my locker which was covered with big red words: GO BACK WHERE YOU BELONG, YOU GOOK.

Nausea flooded my throat, bile so strong my eyes watered. I pushed past Brenda and through the bunch of kids who'd drifted up to stare at my locker and practically ran to the bathroom, where I proceeded to throw up my breakfast.

Last night I'd been attacked by strangers, but this hate was worse. This time it came from people I knew.

Mr. Cheever, our principal, was a small, round, pink-faced man who took any problem that happened in his school as a personal insult. He ordered the janitor to scrub down my locker and asked me if I had any idea who could have done such a thing. I mentioned my run-in with Freckles, whose name I still didn't know. Mr. Cheever then said he'd take care of things and told Brenda to walk me down to the nurse.

Lying down helped my queasy stomach, but everything else proceeded to get worse. First, Kay refused to even talk to me after school, and then, while I was trying to make up with her, Liz ran home, phoned our folks at their realty company, and told them what had happened at school.

Apparently they drove right home, because when I got there, Dad was on the phone talking to Mr. Cheever. "I will not have my daughter harassed," he rumbled. "I want the police called in." He listened to whatever Mr. Cheever was saying and then shouted, "What do you mean, you have no actual *proof* against this Billy Lintell? If you can't handle this, I'll take care of it myself."

Dad was really ripping. His face was almost as red as his hair, and his veins stood out like blue ropes on his forehead and neck. "Watch your blood pressure, Leo," Mom urged, but she looked plenty mad herself.

David now came charging out of his room, waving the semiautomatic toy gun our uncle Martin, who lives in Wisconsin, had sent him for Christmas. "I'll get that creepy Billy Lintell for you, Mai," my kid brother yelled, and shot off his gun—it was so loud, you could swear Rambo himself was in action—almost in Dad's ear.

Dad hung up the phone, took the brat's gun away from him, and then related that Mr. Cheever had apparently questioned Freckles, aka Billy Lintell, but had found no proof that he'd decorated my locker. "I think I'll go over and shake some truth out of the little jerk," Dad announced.

Mom told him to calm down. Dad hollered that he *was* calm. David whined because his toy had been taken away, and Liz just stood there with this scared expression on her face.

I said I had homework and went upstairs to the room Liz and I shared. Once there, I lay down on my bed and stared at the ceiling, where I could still see "Go back where you belong, you gook," printed in huge red letters.

So now you believe me, the voice inside my mind

sighed. *You've always been different and always will be.*

It was what I'd known all my life but had never till now admitted, even to myself. For one thing, such an admission would have made Mom go orbital. She believed wholeheartedly that Different was Good and had this thing about my having a rich cultural heritage. She was really intense about it, insisting that the whole family learn about Vietnam and the Vietnamese culture. She dragged me, and later Liz, to boring museums and lectures. For a while she'd even tried to get us to learn the language, but we were so hopeless at it, she gave up.

Mom also regretted the fact that there were no Asian kids my age in Serena. There were a few other Asian families in town—the Hongs, for example—but their children were much older than me. There was also Morris Woo, but he'd made it plain that he wasn't hanging out with any *girl*, and anyway since he was Chinese American, not Vietnamese, we had nothing in common. So Mom had to be content with the friends I made at school, like Kay.

Kay.

My already-hurting insides ached even more when I thought about the cold look my best friend had given me when I tried to make up with her that afternoon. Intending to try again, I was dialing her number on the phone beside my bed when Mom knocked on the door.

"Are you feeling okay?" she asked worriedly. I lied and said, sure. Mom then came in, shut the door behind her, and walked over to sit on the edge of my bed. "We never did have that talk," she announced.

I turned my head away. "Don't do that," Mom said, an edge in her voice. "You know you can't ever run away from trouble. You have to face up to it."

I felt my eyes go gritty with tears. "They said I should go back where I belong," I whispered.

"Then you're exactly where you belong," my mom said, sure and solid. "You *belong* right here. Besides,

16

who are 'they'? Cowards who don't even dare use their names. They don't matter, Mai."

I knew that I should agree with Mom. If I told her what she wanted to hear, that Billy Lintell was messed in the head and beneath my notice, she would leave me alone.

I started to say, forget it, it's nothing, and instead heard myself say, "Those guys attacked *me* last night, not Liz or Kay."

"You were closest to them, probably," Mom said.

"They came at me because they thought I was Mr. Hong's daughter. They wanted to hurt me because I looked like—like Mai Hongvan," I blurted out.

Mom put her arm around me. "Nobody's going to hurt you."

I hadn't meant that. I wasn't quite sure what I meant. "Did she have any other family?" I heard myself asking. "Mai Hongvan, I mean?"

"One older sister that I know of," Mom said. "Lien Van Tranh arranged your adoption through a friend of ours, the Reverend Anna Tritt, who was working with the refugees in Hong Kong." I could tell Mom didn't know where I was going with this but was prepared to humor me. "I told you all this long ago, remember?"

"I forgot." My tongue felt thick as I tried the unfamiliar name out. "Lien Van Tranh."

"That's right." Mom clasped her hands around her knees and frowned in concentration. "Do you want to hear more about her?"

I hesitated, then nodded.

"I'll tell you what little I know," Mom then said. "Conditions after the Americans left Saigon were terrible. Lien's and Mai Hongvan's father was sent to a reeducation camp and died there. After his death, things got worse. The family escaped by buying passage on a boat run by some profiteer who made money ferrying desperate people out of Vietnam. Mai Hongvan was pregnant with you when she arrived at the refugee camp in Hong Kong."

17

"I remember you telling me that," I muttered.

Mom gave me this thoughtful look. "You never seemed interested in talking about your roots before this," she said, and then told me that it was a hard pregnancy for Mai Hongvan, and that she was tired and sick. "That's why she died soon after you were born."

Part of me wanted to end the story right there, but another part wanted to listen. Mom said that she and Dad had never met Lien.

"Lien approached Anna and told her she wanted her niece to be adopted by an American family," Mom said. "Anna knew that we'd been hoping to adopt a child, so she contacted us. Not that it was easy convincing Lien that we were the right people—she was was very particular about what she wanted for you."

"If she was so particular, why didn't she raise me herself?" I demanded.

"Your father was an American. An Amerasian baby doesn't have an easy time in the Vietnamese community, so Lien felt you'd have a better chance with an American family."

Mom patted my arm as she spoke, but I hardly felt her touch. Instead, I had this weird, disconnected feeling, as if all the people in the world had disappeared and I was all alone.

"What happened to Lien?" I asked.

"The last I heard, she and her husband had emigrated to the States and settled someplace on the East Coast," Mom said. "Boston, I think. Anna had a letter from Lien, years ago, and she told me so on her next Christmas card. That's all I know."

Quiet slid between Mom and me as I thought of Mai Hongvan—really thought about her for the first time in my life. Not just whether I looked like her, but about what she had been like as a girl and how old she'd been when she met the man who'd fathered me. Had she liked blue the way I did? Had she liked listening to music? Had staring into sunlight made her sneeze?

Thinking of Mai Hongvan was like standing at the edge of a really high diving board. I dreaded the dive but at the same time the thought of it was so fascinating that it made me feel dizzy.

Just then there was loud bang downstairs and Liz hollered that Dad had gone out and that the brat had gotten his gun back and was driving her bananas.

Mom hurried off to referee and, left alone, I found I didn't want to think about Mai Hongvan anymore. Instead, I phoned Kay to tell her again that I was sorry. She hung up in my ear.

Next day at school a lot of kids came over to me and told me that they personally despised people who were sick enough to write stuff on lockers. Mr. Cheever had an assembly and got pinker and pinker as he announced that there was no room for prejudice in *his* school.

"All people of whatever race, color, or creed have rights under the Constitution," Mr. Cheever declared. "At Serena High School there will be decency. There will be respect for others' rights. Anyone who steps out of line will be dealt with severely."

Once again I felt as if everybody were looking at me. I sneaked a look at Kay, who was sitting several rows away, and saw her whispering to the girl sitting next to her and pointing at me. Hastily I looked away and saw bony Billy Lintell staring at me in a way that made my stomach go sour.

As a follow-up to his talk, Mr. Cheever called a meeting of the school committee and announced that he'd talked to the police. Both the cops and the teachers at school, our principal declared, were dedicated to tracking down the hate-crime perpetrators. Actually, the said perps weren't discovered either by the teachers or the police, but at least my locker wasn't decorated again.

For a couple of weeks Serena buzzed with talk of

hate crimes but then, luckily, people lost interest in what had happened to me. Part of the reason for this was that the school year was ending and finals were coming. Everybody at school was either cramming or daydreaming about vacation.

Usually Kay and I studied together, but she was still not talking to me, so I studied with Brenda and a couple of other girls. One of them told me that Kay was spreading the word that she hadn't known I was such a weirdo. Maybe, Kay was hinting, this was because Asians hid their true feelings from even their best friends.

Liz told me she'd heard the same thing. "Kay's the one who's weird. She's just jealous because of the attention you've been getting." She sucked her braces thoughtfully. "Luckily we won't have to see her this summer. She's not going to our camp."

Usually, Liz, Kay, and I went to camp at Oswego Lake. Last year Kay and I'd been counselors-in-training, and this year we were going to be counselors. Kay had been looking forward to the job. "Since you know so much, where *is* she going?" I asked.

"I heard her whole family is going to St. Louis to visit her aunt," Liz reported.

I have an aunt, too.

The thought hit me from way out in left field, but I shrugged it away. I had no aunt except Aunt Marilyn, who was married to Uncle Martin and who lived with my two small boy cousins in Aurel, Wisconsin. Lien Van Tranh wasn't really *my* anything. She was only the sister of Mai Hongvan, who had tossed me out of her life because of my mixed blood.

On the morning of our first final—social studies—I got to school early. I was putting some books in my locker and meanwhile reciting the dates I'd memorized when I heard a voice behind me sneer, "Well, well, if it isn't Miss Saigon."

Billy Lintell and a couple of his buddies had come up and were standing behind me. I looked around

20

quickly, but no one else was around. My pulse shot up several notches as I started to walk away.

Billy blocked my path. "What's your hurry?" he demanded.

I snapped, "Get out of my face, Billy Lintell."

"Am I in her face?" Billy asked his sniggering buddies. "Seems like you're in *my* face, Miss Saigon. You, who got me in trouble with Cheever, know that?"

He pushed up close to me. I could smell the faint, sour, sweat smell that came from him, and now I was really scared. With fear tasting hard and metallic in my mouth, I wanted to run—but then remembered Mom's big rule. Don't ever walk away from your fear.

Eyes narrowed, I faced the boy in front of me. "If you don't step out of my way," I snarled, "I'll yell. You want trouble? I'll give you trouble like you won't believe."

"Ooh, she's mad," one of the brainless sidekicks moaned. "Ooh, ooh, I'm scared."

Deliberately, I took a step forward, halving the distance between me and Billy. He didn't budge. With my eyes glued to his bony face, I took another step forward.

Grinning, acting like he'd won some medal for courage, Billy moved aside. I walked past him and then past his buddies, trying to walk slowly and deliberately, while my heart hammered like a kettledrum. As I walked away I heard them sniggering behind me and Billy crooned, "I'm going to get you, gook-face. Whenever you least expect it—expect it."

I was still shaking when I got to my test. I tried to concentrate, but it was no use. My brains felt like mush and all the dates and facts I'd memorized had completely disappeared. When the buzzer went off and I had to hand in my paper, I knew I'd failed a final for the first time in my life.

Afterward I went home and sat around in my room knowing I had to study for my next final but

21

not being able to fix on anything except for what had happened to me that morning and the long summer ahead of me.

Once I'd been happy with campfires and skits and horseback riding, but after today, going to camp seemed pointless. In fact, nothing seemed to have much meaning, not even the things I loved best.

Especially not the things I loved best.

I looked around at my half of the room, at my bulletin board crammed with Four-H ribbons, programs, menus, photos, and mementoes; at my posters of the Doors; at the fuzzy pink teddy bear I'd won at Disneyland. I looked at a photo of me and Kay mugging for the camera.

None of those things seemed to belong to me nor I to them. "Go back where you belong," Billy Lintell had said, but right now I personally had no clue where that might be—

There was a sudden explosion next to my ear that sounded exactly like a gunshot.

Billy—he'd shot me! I screamed and fell off my chair, and as I landed on the floor I heard familiar laughter. "Gotcha!" Brat Houston shrilled.

My kid brother was standing behind me with his stupid toy gun in his hands. "You should see your face," he chortled. "You look like cream cheese!"

I lunged for him and missed. I chased him out of my room and got him on the stairs, but he eeled out of my hands and made tracks downstairs, laughing like a maniac. I got him on the first floor landing and took his gun away and smashed it.

Brat was shrieking at me to stop, and I was cursing him and hollering that if he ever came in my room again, I'd kill him, and then Mom walked through the front door.

"Stop this noise," Mom yelled. In a voice she hardly ever used, she added, "Young lady, you're grounded this weekend for using that language." I shouted, what about *him*, he started it, and Mom ordered me to my room. "I'll deal with your brother," she snapped.

I threw one more insult at Brat and then slammed back into my room. In a little while there were footsteps on the stairs and Mom arrived at my door. No doubt she'd come to tell me never under any circumstances to use such language again, but when she saw my face, she frowned. "What *did* David do to you?" she demanded.

"He shot off that gun thing n-near my ear." In spite of my effort to keep it steady, my voice broke. "I thought he'd c-come after me to sh-shoot me."

"*Shoot* you?" Mom's eyes widened, then narrowed. "Who are you talking about? What happened at school, Mai? Is it Billy Lintell again?" I shrugged, and she said sternly, "Tell me about it right now."

I thought of Billy and his friends and of my failed final. I started to tell Mom about these things and instead blurted out, "I want to go to stay with Lien this summer."

I don't know who was more surprised—me or Mom. She blinked at me. "You what?"

"I don't want to go to camp." For some reason, my voice was rising. "I want to visit Lien Van Tranh. That's what you've always wanted me to do, isn't it, find my roots?"

Mom looked shaken. "I guess I always thought you might want to—but why *now*, Mai?"

How could I possible answer that? The idea of visiting Lien Van Tranh had never occurred to me till now. "I just want to, that's all," I mumbled.

"It's this business with Billy Lintell, isn't it, that has made you think of contacting Lien Van Tranh?" I said nothing. "Baby, you can't just arrive on a stranger's doorstep. It's possible that she may not want to see you."

Mom stopped and waited for me to say something. When I didn't, she continued. "Please think about this, okay? It's an important step for you, and for

23

Lien, too. Besides, I don't know anything about Lien. I don't even know where she is."

Words now burst out of me. "She's on the East Coast, you said, Boston, you said. Your friend Reverend Tritt would know. You know *her* address. You could call her and find out." As Mom opened her mouth to argue, I demanded, "Or do you think that the Tranhs won't accept me because I'm mixed-blooded?"

Mom winced. "That's uncalled for," she exclaimed. "I have no idea what Lien's family will or will not accept. I don't *know* her."

"I don't know her, either—but maybe it's time I did." For some reason my voice had gone shrill, and my heart was thumping like a drum gone crazy. "Why don't you want to let me go? Are you afraid I won't want to come home?"

Mom started to say something, changed her mind, and walked out of the room, slamming the door behind her. I felt a sickening feeling as if I were in an elevator that had just dropped thirty floors.

I wanted to run after Mom and tell her I hadn't meant what I'd said, that I was just hurt and mad and taking it out on her. Instead, I sat where I was and asked myself why I'd suddenly decided I wanted to go and see Lien Van Tranh.

Perhaps it was because I was tired of living with redheads and needed to be around people who looked like me. Or it could be that I craved a friend who accepted me the way I was. Definitely I wanted to see where I'd come from and what made me the way I was.

Mom was wrong. Billy Lintell may have started the avalanche, but all the loose stones had been lying there waiting for a shove.

It hurt to think of Billy, but then, everything else I thought about hurt, too. I just let my mind drift and sat at my desk staring at nothing for half an hour, after which I went downstairs to the kitchen. Mom wasn't around, and David was nowhere to be seen, but Liz was sitting at the counter dunking Oreo cookies in milk. I asked where Mom was, and she cut me a strange look.

"What'd you say to her?" she demanded. I said I didn't want to talk about it. "Well, you really upset her," Liz then declared. She slurped down an Oreo cookie. "You upset David, too."

"*I* upset David?"

"He's just a little kid," Liz said in that snotty way she has. "You know that—but I guess it's not important to you these days."

"What's that supposed to mean?"

"Since you got sprayed with paint you've been acting weird. It's like you think you're the most important person in the world. And now you got David in trouble, too. He's like grounded for life and crying his eyes out, but a fat lot you care."

She slurped another cookie and sucked her braces. "Don't *do* that," I gritted. "It's sickening."

"You're the one that's sickening, Mai Houston. You're not the boss of us, okay?"

Liz glared at me and flounced out of the room just as Mom, holding a piece of paper in her hand, came into the kitchen. She stared at some point over my head as she said in a cool, carefully detached voice, "I managed to reach Anna."

My stomach tightened, and it was suddenly hard to breathe.

"I always knew you'd want to look for your biological family someday," Mom went on, still in that cool voice and still not looking at me. "I have no problem with this and neither does your father. It's the suddenness of it all that worries me. If you're hoping the Tranhs will help you solve your problem with the Billy Lintells of the world, you're not thinking straight."

"That's not why," I muttered, but I couldn't meet her eyes.

Mom handed me the slip of paper. "You'd better write to Lien Van Tranh yourself," she said. "You need to ask her if she *wants* you to visit her. Hearing from you is bound to be a shock after all these years. She may not want to see you or even acknowledge you. It may be that your coming would stir up too many painful memories. If that's the case, you'll have to respect her wishes."

I stared down at the address—408 Springvale Street, Brighton, Massachusetts—and my small trickle of courage ran dry. Maybe I'd better not write, I thought. Maybe I should let this alone. I finally glanced up at my mom and she met my eyes head-on.

It was her I'm-not-running-away-from-trouble stare, but I knew that this time *I* was the one looking for trouble. Mom was right—Lien mightn't want to hear from me. Maybe my writing to her would upset her, disrupt her life.

Suddenly, I was unsure and scared. How would I feel if Lien Van Tranh didn't want any part of me and said so? But then again—what if she'd been hoping, waiting for word from me all these years?

"What should I do?" I whispered.

But Mom had already walked out of the kitchen, and I was on my own. I looked back down at Lien Van Tranh's address on the paper in my hand.

A letter, I thought. How could one letter hurt?

Chapter Three

I MUST HAVE destroyed a ton of paper before I finally managed to write a short note telling Lien who I was. I asked her if I could come and visit her in Boston, added that if she didn't want me, I understood, and that was okay with me. Then I stamped the envelope, dropped it into the mailbox, and immediately felt as if I'd done the dumbest thing in the world.

That letter to Lien haunted me. I thought about it constantly. Dreamed about it. Each time the phone rang, I jumped, and each day I nearly broke my neck running to check the mailbox. Liz told me to please quit acting like loony tunes, and David started sneaking up behind me to croon, "Ma-ail's co-oming, Mai!" just to see how high I'd jump.

Mom and Dad ignored all of this. They pretended that everything was cool, but even in my agitated state I knew this was far from true. Things at the Houstons *seemed* normal all right—school ending, Liz packing for camp, the folks busy with a new listing to which they'd got the exclusive—but the rhythm wasn't right. We were like people singing a familiar song slightly off-key.

Then, right after the Fourth of July, which Serena celebrated with its annual town parade complete with fire engines and the Serena High marching band, I came home from picking up milk at the store and found Mom sitting at the kitchen table. It was the middle of the day and she was all dressed for the office, but she was just sitting. There wasn't even a cup of coffee in front of her or paperwork or anything.

"Is everything okay?" I asked, worried.

"Lien just telephoned me," Mom told me.

My throat went dry, and I had to swallow before I could croak, "What did she say?"

"She said that she'd received your letter." Mom was carefully casual as she went on. "I gather you asked if you could spend the summer with her family in Boston."

I swallowed again, but no words of explanation came out of my sandpaper throat. Mom said, "Lien was sorry she hadn't replied to your letter before. Apparently the Tranhs have all been busy at the family restaurant. Lien's nephew from Vietnam is coming to the States to attend medical school, and the Tranhs are working night and day to help pay for his expenses."

I felt a rush of disappointment just barely tinged with relief. "So she doesn't want me to come."

Mom took in a deep breath that wasn't quite a sigh. "What Lien *said* was that you were welcome to visit Boston provided you didn't mind pitching in at the Mua Xuan Restaurant. She left her number. It's there by the phone."

Legs rubbery, I walked over to the phone and stared down at the number on the scratch pad. All I had to do was dial this number, but now I hesitated. "What did she sound like? I mean, what kind of person do you think—"

"It's hard to say over the phone." Mom was definitely not going to make it easier for me. "I suggest you find out for yourself."

She then got up and walked out of the kitchen, leaving me staring at the phone. It was like a movie script: After years of trying to locate her birth family, the heroine tracks them down. Now she stands, phone in hand, her heart pounding like a drum, but she can't make her fingers punch those numbers. Fi-

28

nally, with a supreme effort of will, she does it. A dial tone whirs. Clicks. Now she waits.

One ring, two, three, four—and a clear, bright voice sang, "Mua Xuan Restaurant." I stammered that I was looking for Lien Van Tran. "This is Nancy, her daughter. Can I help you?"

I had a blood cousin called Nancy! She sounded about my age and friendly, too. I stammered, "This is Mai Houston. From Serena, Iowa. I wrote—"

There was a crash in the background and someone commenced yelling in what I guessed was Vietnamese. "I'm sorry," Nancy apologized, "I didn't catch what you said. My brother just dropped a whole tray of plates. I'll go get Ma for you, okay?"

I didn't have time to digest the fact that I also had a boy cousin, before a new voice spoke into the receiver. "Lien here," it said. "Who's this?"

My birth aunt's voice was husky and deep. She tossed her few words out quickly as if grudging the time it took to say them. When I told her who I was, she went, "You come to Boston."

She didn't make it sound like an invitation or even a question. It was more like an order thrown casually over her shoulder at the cook. You know: one Buddha's Delight to go. I said cautiously, "Do you *want* me to come?"

"Sure," replied my newfound aunt promptly. "You can come. Family all working at restaurant so Gian Cu can come over and study to be doctor here in USA. Nguyen, Vinh, all work. Can use extra pair of hands."

She broke off to issue a rapid-fire volley of Vietnamese commands, then said, "Can't talk now. Tell me what you decide to do, okay?" and hung up.

As I was staring at the receiver in my hand, Mom came back into the kitchen and looked me squarely in the eye. I knew that expression well; it was her meet-trouble look. "Well?" she went. "Does she want you to come?"

Lien hadn't sounded welcoming, but at least she'd

29

said I could come if I liked. She'd also talked about my working with "the family," which hopefully meant that she considered me part of the clan. I pictured my blood family, all dark-haired and dark-eyed like me. I thought of Nancy (or, Nguyen?) and her brother (Vinh?), cousins I had never even known existed until now.

Go back where you belong, gook.

With Billy Lintell's voice nudging my mind, I said, "I want to go to Boston."

"Fine," Mom said. "I'll call Adele Fine at Travel Right and have her book two flights to Logan Airport in Boston."

"I don't need you to come with me," I protested, but that made my mom look even more determined.

"You didn't think I'd let you go alone, did you?"

I explained to Mom that I was practically sixteen and able to fly across the country without a chaperon, that my going to Boston was something I needed to do by myself for myself, so please, could she respect my space? *Mom* said that if I thought she was going to allow her daughter to fly across the country to stay with a family she'd never laid eyes on, I didn't know her very well. Then *I* told her I didn't need her to nursemaid me, that I knew what I was doing, and why couldn't she trust me, anyway? to which she gritted, "Really? I must say you're not acting very mature right now."

We got into this really bad argument which Mom capped by declaring that I was acting like a spoiled brat. "Either we do it my way," she announced, "or we won't do it at all."

I slammed into Liz's and my room, where I threw myself on my bed and I proceeded to pound my pillow the way I'd done when I was a little kid. Part of me knew I was acting like a brat, but I was too frustrated to care. The bottom line was that I didn't want Mom coming with me to Boston. As I'd said, meeting the Tranhs was something I needed to do for myself, by myself.

I stayed in my room till Mom left the house. She and Dad were at work till late, and David was sleeping over at a friend's from his day camp, so I was alone all day. I told myself I was glad about it, that I didn't want to have to deal with anybody right now, but to be honest, it felt as if I were being quarantined. As if my decision to visit Lien had cut me off from the rest of the family.

Next morning when I came downstairs, Mom announced stiffly that she'd phoned the Van Tranhs. "We agreed that you'd fly down to Boston day after tomorrow, which would make it Thursday, the seventh," she said. "I'll fly east with you, stay the night, and return on Friday. I understand that this is your show, and you needn't worry that I'll interfere in any way."

My mom delivered all this information in a crisp tone that told me she was still plenty mad about what we'd said to each other yesterday. A part of me was grateful she'd made all the arrangements, but another part of me resented it. I should have been the one to phone Lien, make plans about my own life.

"What about that house you're showing?" I muttered, but Mom said that I wasn't to worry—that Dad could hold the fort.

"I have a morning appointment with a client," she then said, and left. No hug, no "See you later, baby," not even a smile, and the house went so quiet and lonely that even my playing Aerosmith at top volume couldn't drown it out.

So I shut off the music and let silence follow me as I found my suitcase and carried it up to my room— silence that asked me what I was trying to prove, anyway, and why was I acting like such a jerk— silence that was fractured when the telephone started to ring.

When I picked up the receiver, an agitated voice exclaimed, "Mrs. Houston?" I said, no, it was her daughter. "I've tried her office but couldn't reach her or Mr. Houston," the woman then screeched. "This is Mrs. Glosse, the nurse at the Sundale Day Camp. David has had an accident. We're afraid his leg is broken."

I reached Mom on her car phone and told her that David had been taken to Owen Johns Hospital. She said that she'd swing by the house and pick me up, but I told her that'd take too long and that I'd ride my bike to the hospital and meet her there.

Though Serena was a small town, we were lucky in our hospital. Owen Johns was a teaching hospital, very modern and efficient, the best in the county. Hospital personnel directed me to the X-ray waiting room, where I found Mom staring sightlessly at some TV talk show.

"The doctor thinks David has fractured his tibia," she told me. "They're taking X rays now."

Then she added distractedly, "I've just now managed to reach your father. He was with a client all this time and out of reach of the car phone."

I asked how bad David's leg was, but before Mom could answer, they wheeled the brat in on a gurney. He looked white and scared, and his mouth was twitching and twisting as if he were fighting tears, but he managed a ghost of a grin at me. "You should see the other guy," he went, and suddenly I wanted to cry.

Mom looked ready to cry, too, when the osteopathic surgeon said they wanted to keep David at the hospital for today, at least. She kept patting my brother's shoulder and saying he'd be okay. We were a pretty miserable crew when Dad came striding in, demanding to know what had happened to his son.

They gave David something for the pain, and he soon fell into a twitchy sleep. We all stayed at the hospital till late afternoon. Then Dad drove home to collect some stuff for David, and Mom said I should go, too.

"I'll stay and eat at the cafeteria, but please start

some supper for Dad," she directed. Then she added, "Mai, we have a problem."

My stomach twisted with apprehension, and I shot an anxious look at the pale, fitfully sleeping huddle that was my brother. Did she know something about David that I didn't? But then Mom said, "I won't be able to fly to Boston with you."

Till she said that, I swear, I'd forgotten all about Lien and the Tranhs. Maybe Mom read that thought in my eyes, because her expression softened.

"I haven't been fair to you, baby," she sighed. "I should have been more understanding. It's just that I'm really afraid that you're doing the wrong thing by going to Boston *now*."

She reached out, patted my hand. "It's been an—an emotional time for all of us, hasn't it? When things settle down, you and I need to sit down and talk about this. But now isn't the time."

I knew she was worried about me, and I knew what I *should* say. If I offered to postpone my trip, the rift between Mom and me would heal. I nearly said the words that would make everything okay between us, but then thought of Lien waiting for me. I thought of the two blood cousins I'd never known existed. If I canceled my plans now, would they want me to come to Boston another time?

I couldn't be sure that they would. "If you're set on going ahead with this," Mom was saying, "Dad will drive you to Cedar Rapids. You'll have to change planes in Minneapolis, but someone from the airline will direct you, and it's not a long flight. Lien will meet you at Logan Airport in Boston."

She paused and looked hopefully at me. Last chance, Mai—but I'd gone too far to draw back.

"Okay," I told Mom. "I'll call Lien tonight."

Lien said that she'd be wearing a pink blouse when she came to meet me at Logan Airport. I was relying on that blouse because I was totally clueless about what my blood aunt looked like. I hadn't thought to

33

ask her for a photo, and she hadn't described herself at all.

So, once I walked out into the waiting area at Logan, I looked around for an Asian lady in a pink blouse. For a while, no one fit the bill and my stomach was beginning to twist into sour knots when I saw a woman pushing through the crowd toward me. A short, lean, rawboned Asian woman who was wearing a shocking pink blouse over black pants— "Lien Van Tranh?" I hazarded to say.

She looked around her and spotted me. She had a long, narrow, high-cheekboned face framed with a frizz of permed hair, and her wide-set black eyes watched me unwinkingly from behind rimless glasses. As she began to stride purposefully toward me, she didn't open her arms wide and shout, "Mai, Mai," or even crack a smile. In fact, her mouth remained folded tight.

"Toi roi!"

I blinked uncomprehendingly at her, and her lips folded into an even grimmer line. "You don't speak Vietnamese, ha?" she demanded. "I say, there you are. Plane was late."

While I was mumbling that I was sorry, she looked me up and down. "You don't look like anyone in the family," she accused.

I started to apologize again but caught myself in time. Why should I apologize for not looking like people I'd never seen before today? But at the same time, I felt a stir of disappointment. I'd always figured that I favored Mai Hongvan's side of the family.

"We go get your suitcase," Lien was announcing in her gruff, clip-and-throw fashion. "Nguyen is waiting outside. Save on parking that way. Logan is horrible expensive for parking."

She marched off toward the luggage claim area, leaving me to trail after her, which I did. Was Nancy-Nguyen like her mother? My stomach nervous-cramped at the thought, and I held my breath until we got outside the terminal, where a

34

battered old pickup was idling. A girl, her long black hair rippling in the warm wind, stuck her head out of the window to shout, "Hurry, Ma—if I stay here any longer, they'll ticket us."

"Inside," Lien commanded me. She grabbed my suitcase, tossed it into the back of the pickup, and got in the front seat. "Nguyen, move over so I can drive. You—get in beside Nguyen."

I hopped into the pickup, and with a wheezing rattle it took off. My cousin squeezed herself sideways and said, "Hi, Mai. I'm Nancy." She held out a small hand tipped with pearly nails for me to take and added, "I'm glad you made it."

The genuine pleasure in her voice caused my nerves to ease a little. "So'm I," I began. "I thought—"

"Time to pay toll," Lien's gruff voice interrupted. "You get dollar out of my purse, Nguyen. You talk so much, you forget, ha?"

Nancy rolled her eyes at me but did as she was told, and as we rode along, I admired her profile. She had Lien's lean bone structure, but on her the high cheekbones were beautiful.

My newfound cousin had an almost perfectly oval face, pale ivory skin, and almond-shaped eyes that snapped with spirit. Her small ears had tiny gold and jade studs in them. She had a curved bow of a mouth that was pink without lipstick, and she smiled as she turned to me again.

"Me and Vinny have been dying to meet you ever since you wrote," she told me.

"Me, too," I said. I wanted to ask Nancy if she'd known about me, if Lien had told her, but somehow my aunt's silent presence held me back. So I asked, testing the unfamiliar name, "Where is—Vinny?"

"Vinh at restaurant," Lien declared. "He work."

Once more she sounded accusing, as if having to pick me up at the airport was keeping her from the restaurant. I sat back and kept quiet while my aunt wove us in and out of traffic. I watched the Boston skyline, amazed at how tall the buildings looked to be, and hoped that the rest of the family was more like Nancy than Lien.

Used to small-town Serena, I stared at Boston like any hick from the country. Parts of the city were really, really beautiful and grand, and the rest of it looked depressed. "Commonwealth Avenue," Nancy announced as we turned into a wide, tree-lined street divided in the middle by streetcar tracks. "It's not far now."

A green and white streetcar rattled past. Lien's old pickup slowed, then made a turn onto a nearly treeless street crowded with shops and lots of people. Students, old people, mothers with babies, Latinos, Asians, caucasians, African Americans—all of them were walking or strolling or chatting or shopping. "Harvard Avenue," Nancy told me.

Excellent bakery smells filled the air as we drove past Lou's Bakery, disappeared near Woolworth's. We rattled past a deli and the Korean market, a barbershop, a furniture store, and slowed at the red and blue neon sign of an electronics store called Megabytes.

As we made a turn into Springvale Street, a skinny kid waved at us from Megabytes' doorway. "Hey, Tommy," Nancy leaned across me to call. "Tommy Vuong has been Vinny's best friend since all the way back in kindergarten."

Lien muttered something under her breath, and I saw that across the street from Megabytes was a building with a bright green pagoda for a roof. "Is that your restaurant?" I asked.

Lien snorted. Nancy explained, "That's the Jade Palace—a Chinese restaurant. It just opened a month ago. Our place is over there."

I blinked at a postage-stamp of a restaurant wedged between the Siamese Video Mart and a dry cleaner. Through the sparkling but tiny window I could see an elderly man dozing in one of the few booths, while a young couple was eating under a bright red and gold butterfly on the wall.

"There is Mua Xuan," Lien was saying proudly. "Dinner crowd not here yet."

"*If* it ever gets here," Nancy added pointedly.

Lien scowled. "Nguyen, go park pickup. You, take suitcase upstairs." She hopped out of the pickup and then added to Nancy, "Come right back, hear me? Don't hang around, talk people on way back."

I saw my cousin's lips tighten, and for a second she looked a lot like Lien. Then, wordlessly, she put the pickup in gear and drove off. "We buy pickup when we start restaurant," Lien said in a satisfied tone. "More useful than car. Come with me now, I show you where you sleep."

She led the way around to the back of the building, where a flight of stone stairs led to a green metal door. Lien unlocked this door and led me into a dark, narrow entryway. On one side of this hall were some more stairs. On the other side stood a door through which I could hear the clatter of plates and the wail of a flute.

"Restaurant is through that door," Lien said. "It's not locked, you can go in later. Now I take you upstairs to apartment, so you can put your suitcase in your room."

Food smells followed me as I climbed the dark stairs, and my stomach growled. I wondered if Lien would offer me something to eat, but all she said was "We live here."

"Here" was another door which Lien unlocked using two keys. It swung open into a tiny linoleum-floored kitchen with a gleaming white refrigerator and stove. In a wall alcove near the door stood a golden Buddha surrounded by incense, a bowl of rice, apples, and a pack of cigarettes. On the refrigerator a magnetic frame showed a photo of a young Vietnamese guy with glasses and an old-fashioned Beatles-type haircut.

"Nephew," Lien explained. "Gian Cu is in Ho Chih

Minh City now. He waiting for his request to leave Vietnam to be processed, but government takes too long time."

Had her voice softened as she spoke of this nephew? Would she meet him with more enthusiasm than she had greeted me? I tried not to think of this as Lien led me into a small room crammed with a TV set, a table, and chairs. Farther on was a hall and four closed doors.

"Bathroom," Lien announced. "You want use? Next door is bedroom for Vinh and Cousin Pham. Next come Nguyen's room. You stay here with her."

My shared bedroom was tiny compared to Liz's and my room back home, but I told myself I wasn't here to make comparisons. Instead, I concentrated on the friendly pink curtains hanging at the windows, a cluttered dresser with a mirror, a closet bulging with clothes, sneakers, and shoes, a pennant that said HARVARD CRIMSON on it, and a Nirvana poster.

Bunk beds had been wedged into the small space. I was touched. Though not overly demonstrative, Lien had wanted me to come and had prepared a bed for me.

"Cousin Luu live with us till you come," Lien explained, shattering this delusion. "She stay now with the Ding family."

Was I supposed to feel guilty because I'd displaced still another cousin? I eyed Lien uncertainly, but my newfound aunt just directed me to unpack, get changed, use the bathroom, and come on downstairs to the restaurant. To meet the others? to work? I wasn't sure, and I didn't dare ask.

Not knowing what else to do, I changed from my traveling jeans into another pair of jeans and used the bathroom—a tiny room which was totally, but *totally* crammed with an old claw-footed bathtub, commode, and sink, and a huge shelf lined with jars and tins and paper bags with Vietnamese writing all over them—and then went downstairs to the Mau Xuan Restaurant.

The hall door opened into the restaurant kitchen. It was small, narrow, dark, and smelled of garlic, fish, citrus, and spice. A long counter ran down each side, and at this counter was a small man who was grasshopper-skinny everywhere but in his round middle. He was wrapped up in a huge white apron and had a white cap on top of his head. He was leaning over a counter and whacking away at some ribs with a humongous cleaver.

A younger man, the sprout of his mustache resting uneasily over a down-curved mouth, was slicing vegetables. A fat woman was frying something in a huge pan. All of them were listening to the wailing flute music.

"Don't just stand there, Mai. Come meet everyone."

Nancy had just walked through the swinging doors that apparently separated the kitchen from the restaurant. Having seen her only sitting down, I was surprised at how tiny she was. About five feet tall, she looked slender and graceful in her flowing black skirt and white blouse. Next to her, I felt like a horse, especially now that everyone was staring my way.

"This is Mai Houston, who just arrived from Iowa," Nancy announced, then paused to speak in what had to be Vietnamese. "Cousin Luu doesn't speak much English," she explained.

The fat lady—so this was the Cousin Luu I'd driven out to go live with the Ðing family—nodded and grinned at me, showing a gold tooth. She said something that sounded like, *"Tok, tok,"* which made the young guy with the mustache suspend his chopping long enough to check me out.

The older man with the white cap spoke in a voice that reminded me of a bird cheeping. "Hel-lo," he said. "What you think about Boston?"

"She just got here, Papa." Nancy walked over to

39

me with an easy grace I could have died for, and, sliding an arm through mine, urged me farther into the room. "Mai, this is my dad—your uncle Diep. And here is another cousin. Pham's pre-law at Northeastern University."

Pham grunted. Small eyes, as welcoming as black ice chips, lingering on me for another minute and then slid disgustedly away. I felt my cheeks grow hot at his rudeness as my uncle whispered, "Want eat something? Drink some *tra*, maybe?"

"Good idea, Papa," Nancy said. She walked over to one of the counters and poured dark liquid into a cup. "Here you go," she said. "Enjoy it."

They all watched curiously as I took a sip. "You like Vietnamese tea?" Uncle Diep wanted to know.

I nodded. It was like the tea I'd had at Chinese restaurants. "Luu's frying up a batch of Grandma Bach Thi's secret spring rolls," Nancy was saying. "They're the specialty of the house—guaranteed to bring you back for more. But maybe after your flight and everything, you're not hungry right now."

"I can eat anytime," I confessed.

"Obviously. You're a *growing* girl."

Pham's voice was high, nasal, and when he laughed he sounded like a whinnying horse. Ignoring him, I said, "Everything at the Mau Xuan smells delicious."

Pham chuckled nastily at my pronunciation and Nancy said, "You can call it the Spring Restaurant if you like." She paused to look me up and down. "So, long-lost cousin, for sure we don't look alike."

This was the second time today I'd been told this. "Lien—ah, *Aunt* Lien—told me that I didn't look like anyone in the family." Not wanting Pham to hear, I lowered my voice to add, "She said that I didn't look like Mai Hongvan, either."

"I wouldn't know about that—I've never seen a picture of Aunt Mai." Nancy's dark eyes sparkled with curiosity as she added, "When you wrote, we were all real surprised. I mean, all these years,

40

nothing, and then—out of the clear blue sky, boom! Here you are. I mean, it's great, but it's kind of a shock, too."

"You didn't know I was living in Iowa?" I asked. Nancy shook her head.

"We didn't know about you at all—no, wait, I take that back. When I was in fifth grade, I was drawing this family tree for school. Papa said that I should put Aunt Mai in, and then he said something about Mai's baby. But then Ma told him to quit talking about it because it—you, I mean—had been adopted by an American family. That's all she told us."

So Nancy and Vinny hadn't known about me—but then, I hadn't known much about them, either. It was unreal. Here I was, talking about my birth mother to a cousin I'd never known existed till a few days ago.

I watched Nancy slip on an apron and start helping her father dip the ribs in a thick paste and then drop them into a smoking pan of oil. *Un*real. Just this morning I'd been in Serena, trying to tame the butterflies in my stomach while eating cereal from my old, familiar cereal bowl and listening to Mom say—in that controlled voice she used when talking to me these days—that I should phone her when I landed in Boston. "We just want to know you're safe," she had added. "After that I promise not to bother you."

I was about to tell Nancy I had to call Serena, when the swinging doors behind me parted and an Asian guy walked in. He was around eighteen, and he was built lean and mean. A white mesh T-shirt showed off shoulders and forearms arms that bulged with muscle, and he wore tight black jeans. A black pearl bobbed in his left ear.

"Hey, old uncle," he called.

Diep kept whacking at the ribs, but I saw that his ears were turning red. Nancy demanded, "What do you want, Sammy Vuong?"

Whoever Sammy Vuong was, I liked him even less

41

than I liked Pham, maybe because he somehow reminded me of Billy Lintell. "I just stopped to say a friendly hello," he was saying.

"I'll bet. And I suppose you stopped at the Jade Palace on your way here?"

Ignoring Nancy, Sammy turned to me. "What do we have here, a new waitress? You a Filipina, baby?"

"Don't pay any attention to him, Mai," Nancy told me, and Sammy grinned.

"Oh-ho," he said. "So this is the *con lai*."

Diep muttered something in Vietnamese. Sammy Vuong's grin didn't waver, but his eyes grew meaner. "*Can than*, old uncle—be careful. One word from me to the *dai lo*, and you and your chickenshit restaurant'll be history. We won't always be so nice to you just because my little brother hangs out with your son."

He reached out, snagged a rib from the plate, and started chewing. "The Jade Temple's doing good," he went on. "Next time this week, all your customers could be going there."

Diep, ears now red as beetroots, snapped, "You get out of here."

"Yeah, why don't you take off—" but the words were hardly out of Pham's mouth before Sammy whirled, grabbed him by the shirt, and hauled him almost over the counter.

"What's that you said, dirtbag?"

Pham's eyed bulged. His face got red and then purple, and he made gargling noises in his throat. Cousin Luu clenched her hands together and whispered, *"Xau, xau,"* to herself. No one moved, not even Uncle Diep, and I stared, hypnotized like the rest as Sammy snarled, "I should smash your head for dissing me."

"You get out of here!"

I swiveled around to see Lien striding through the swinging doors. "You go now or I call police," she commanded.

"The cops won't do anything for you," Sammy Vuong sneered. "You keep out of this, old lady."

Lien darted across the room, grabbed Uncle Diep's meat cleaver, pivoted to face Sammy. "Let go of Pham and get out."

Sammy's eyes narrowed fractionally, and his nostrils flared. He glared down at Lien, who was by now waving that meat cleaver under his nose. For a second their eyes locked, and it was Sammy who looked away.

"I don't have time for you," he snarled. He let go of Pham, who sank wheezing down behind the counter and put his hands in his pockets. "I'll be back."

Lien spat out a string of Vietnamese words as Sammy Vuong banged his way through the swinging doors. "Diep, you go now. Make sure that one leaves the restaurant without making trouble," she ordered.

Then she glared at the rest of us and spat out a question which had to mean "What are you standing around for?"

Right away, everybody got busy. Uncle Diep scurried off through the swinging doors. Cousin Luu kept on frying spring rolls. Pham, still hacking and rasping, returned to chopping his vegetables.

Only Nancy stayed where she was. "Ma," she said, "you shouldn't have done that. Sammy could've hurt you. You know he runs with the Pearls."

"What you want me to do? Pay that worthless boy protection money?" Lien demanded. "Never happens. I know Sammy Vuong since he was in diaper. Our families leave Vietnam together."

"That Jade Palace restaurant down the street is making good money and taking a lot of our customers," Nancy persisted. "They're paying the Pearls what they want, that's why. Sammy Vuong's a punk, but he's got a lot of muscle behind him, Ma. You *know* Ly's fruit store wouldn't pay the Pearls, and look what happened to them. So far they've only broken our front window, but—"

"Enough!" Lien decreed. "Nguyen, you go into restaurant now, talk to customers." Her eyes roamed the kitchen, settled on me. "You can help Nguyen set up tables."

"Will you give it a rest, Ma?" Nancy protested. "Mai just got here, okay. She was just having some tea."

"Tea?" Lien repeated. It was as if she'd never heard the word before. "Okay," she then grudged, "you finish *tea*. If you tired, you can go upstairs and rest."

Withered by her scorn, I spoke quickly. "I'm not tired," I said. "I can work."

I'd come to Boston prepared to pitch in at the Mua Xuan. Besides, having seen Lien in action just now, I was determined to stay on her good side. My blood aunt was one tough lady, and no way was I about to cross her.

Chapter Four

LIEN'S THIN LIPS stretched in what I guess was an approving smile. "Okay. You can help Vinh clear tables."

As if on cue, a teenaged boy came backing through the swinging doors, a tray loaded with dishes balanced in his long arms. He turned his head to look at me and tripped over his own big feet.

"Hey, Vinny, watch it!" Nancy warned.

Vinny did this crazy juggling act and managed to keep the plates and bowls from sliding off the teetering tray. "Stupid," Lien scolded. "How many time I tell you, watch where you going?"

My younger cousin set down the tray and pushed dark hair out of his eyes. He was a year or so older than Liz and almost as tall as me. He had a round, olive-dark, serious face, but when he grinned at me, there was a dimple at the corner of his mouth. Lien announced, "This Mai Houston. She help you clear the tables."

He sort of waggled his fingers at me. "Hi," I said, self-conscious myself, and he asked politely how my flight had been.

Lien wasn't about to let this conversation go anywhere. "Time to talk later," she told us. "Nguyen, customer just come in. Go take order." Then picking up a wet rag and slapping it into my hands she added, "Come. I show how to wipe down and set up table."

Even though only a half-dozen customers trickled in all evening, Lien wouldn't let me stand still for a second. When there were no tables that demanded my attention, she had me wash the kitchen floor, scrub counters, and rinse off plates for the old-fashioned dishwasher. Toward the end of the evening, my arms and shoulders ached.

I asked Nancy if her mother ever believed in resting, and she laughed at me as if I were nuts. "Not the Woman of Steel. Ten minutes to closing time, and she's still hoping for the big dinner rush."

Vinny went through the swinging doors just then, and I caught a glimpse of Lien standing by the door of the restaurant and peering up the street. Only two people remained inside the Mua Xuan. They'd long-ago finished eating but were dawdling over their tea, and the kitchen was starting to close down. Pham, wearing the sourest expression known to man, was washing pots. Cousin Luu was scrubbing the stove. Uncle Diep was cleaning his knives as carefully as if they were made of gold.

"Come outside for a few seconds," Nancy told me. "You look ready to drop dead or something. Quick—while Ma's not around to catch us."

She motioned me out of the kitchen door and led the way through the hall and out the green metal door. Warm, fresh wind had never felt so good, until I nearly choked on the gas fumes of a car passing by.

"Air quality here isn't that great," Nancy agreed, "but you ain't seen nothin' yet. Wait till it gets hot in August. You're crazy, you know," she added. "Most people are dying to get *out* of this city in the summer."

She sat down on the lowest back step and pushed her flowing hair out of her eyes. "I *hate* this hairstyle," she moaned. "I'd cut it all off, but Ma would take a fit. She thinks young Vietnamese girls should look fragile and innocent."

She leaned back and stared up at the sky where, undaunted by the heavy air, a couple of dim stars were hanging out. "Do you smoke?"

I explained that since my mom had given up the weed ten years ago, she'd been a total fanatic about not getting addicted to nicotine. "Too bad," Nancy sighed. "I'm dying for a smoke."

I could hear Lien's voice rising from the kitchen and wondered if she was looking for us. "I don't care what she wants," my cousin then declared, "I am not going back in there. I've had it with hauling *bahn phong tom* and *ga uop chao nuong*, for lousy ten percent tips, and if I smell that damned fish sauce again, I'll throw up." She added fretfully, "I wish to God that Gian Cu weren't coming. Then we wouldn't have to be working ourselves to death."

"Why do you have to?" I asked cautiously.

"It's one of Ma's obsessions," Nancy said. She narrowed her eyes, scrunched up her mouth, and mimicked Lien's spit-and-throw speech. "Gian is family. We must help family. Is our duty."

Apparently, this Gian Cu was a cousin on Lien's side. His family had stayed in Vietnam and survived the war, and now he wanted to come to America to study medicine. To help Gian achieve this goal, the Tranhs had actually taken out a bank loan.

"Gian Cu wants to become a doctor and then go back to Vietnam and help the folks at home," Nancy explained.

I said that you had to admire the guy. Nancy snorted. "Tell me that when Ma gets you up at six tomorrow."

I stared at her. "Six in the *morning*? Be real! What could be so important that you have to get up at six?"

"She's got the refugee work ethic," Vinny said. He'd come bobbing through the green door and now plopped down on the top step behind us. "Worse than those Puritans on the *Mayflower*. Work, work work. Save, save, save. Family, family, family. Don't stop to take a breath or the boogeyman'll get you."

Vinny didn't sound mad like Nancy. He just sounded weary and resigned. I thought of me and Liz spending our summer at Camp Oswego and complaining about mosquitoes and the boring camp food. "But once Gian Cu comes over, you guys can relax," I pointed out.

"Before Gian there was Luu, and before that there

47

was Pham." Nancy's voice turned bitter. "When I think of how we slaved to bring that mean-mouthed, stuck-up creep over here, I could throw up."

From the little I'd seen of Pham, I tended to agree. I asked what Pham's problem was, and Nancy said attitude. "He's the only son of Papa's dead brother, and I guess his mother spoiled him rotten. Pham believes he's the smartest person in the world."

"He *is* smart," Vinny added, "but mean. No way would I ever turn my back on that dude. Anyway, after Gian gets here, we'll probably be working to bring Luu's kids over."

I guess I looked surprised. Vinny explained, "Luu—she's Papa's first cousin—got cleared to come over a year ago, but her husband and kids are still back in 'Nam. Ma's helping her save to get them over here."

"That'll take forever," Nancy said. "Luu works for minimum wage. She could be an illegal, the way Ma treats her." She chewed on that thought for a moment, and then burst out, "She never lets up, you know? First it was save like crazy to get the restaurant. Then we needed money to pay off the bank loans. It'll never end."

Vinny got to his feet, stretched, and announced that he was going over to a friend's. Nancy said he was nuts. "It's past ten, you dummy."

"Tommy's got that new video game—Deathworld. He'll still be playing. If Ma asks, tell her I've already gone to bed, 'kay?"

Vinny loped down the stairs, all long legs and elbows and angles. Nancy hissed after him, "If you don't get back here in an hour, your ass is grass, boy." Then, as her brother disappeared, she shook her head. "If Ma knew he was going to see Tommy Vuong, she'd kill him."

"Because of Sammy?" I asked.

"Smart girl—you get an A and move to the head of the class. Sammy runs with the Pearls—he was jumped in this spring, and he already acts as if he's

48

the *dai lo*—gang leader. Mrs. Vuong cries, Mr. Vuong prays to Buddha. A fat lot of good that does."

Nancy's voice cracked with scorn. I was about to ask who the Pearls were, when Lien stuck her head out of the door.

"What you girls doing out there?" she demanded suspiciously. "Where Vinh?"

"In bed, of course." The lie slid so easily off Nancy's lips that I knew she'd had plenty of practice. "A growing boy needs his sleep, Ma."

"And you not growing, ha?" A passing car illuminated Lien's frizz of hair and hatchet-lean face, and I saw that she was looking at me with a strange expression in her eyes. For a moment it seemed as if she were going to come out with something important, but she just said, "You better go to sleep, now. Long trip you made today. Must be tired."

It wasn't the *trip* that had made me so tired, I could have said, but I didn't have the nerve. I got to my feet, but Nancy stayed put. "Nguyen," Lien urged.

"I'll get there, Ma." There was an edge to Nancy's voice as she added, "Don't rush me, okay? I want to sit here for a while and look at the sky."

"Sky is overcast," Lien snorted. "Nothing to see here in the city."

Nancy tossed back her hair and started to hum under her breath. Lien scowled at her for a moment, then clicked her tongue and held the door open for me. "You," she said firmly, "come."

I climbed the stairs slowly, hoping Nancy would follow. She didn't, and my respect for my older cousin rose. To stand up to her mother took guts.

But she had also lied to Lien—for a second the Houston taboo against all manner and form of deception touched my mind, then it slid away. If Mom was like Lien Van Tranh, I reasoned, I'd probably be telling a few whoppers myself.

I meant to stay awake till Nancy came to bed, but the next thing I knew, an alarm clock was shrilling

49

in the near distance. I rolled over and peered at the
clock behind my bed and groaned.

My aunt Lien was getting up at five in the morning.
You could hear her feet hitting the bare floor, and
shortly afterward she passed our room on her way to
the shower. It was a quickie—by five-ten she was telling Uncle Diep to get up. By a quarter to six she was
hassling Pham and Vinny. Then it was our turn.

Why? I wondered as I showered quickly in the by-
now-cold water and waited my turn to dry my hair,
since two hair dryers going at once would blow all the
fuses in the house. The restaurant didn't even open
till eleven, and from what I'd seen yesterday, there
wouldn't be any crowds beating down the door. So why
did we have to get up at the crack of dawn?

But this was Lien Van Tranh's house, where normal laws didn't apply. From the moment we came
out into the room with the table and chairs, there
was work to do. While Uncle Diep fiddled with the
incense in front of the Buddha in the kitchen, breakfast had to be put on the table. Vinny and Nancy and
I opted for cereal, but Lien cooked up rice, soup, and
a dish of green veggies stir-fried with meat for Diep,
Pham, and herself.

Finally we sat down to breakfast and I picked up
my spoon, only to find Lien's disapproving eyes
honed on me. What had I done now? I wondered, until Nancy kicked me lightly under the table and said,
"Enjoy your food, Ma. Papa."

Pham parroted Nancy, as did Vinny. "Enjoy it," Lien
grated, but kept her eyes hard on me. Only when I'd
followed Nancy's lead did Lien look away from me.

She acted as though I'd made some unforgivable
social blunder. How was I supposed to know what to
do or say? I asked myself later as I helped wash
breakfast dishes, sweep the apartment, and make
beds. Then the bathroom had to be scrubbed, and I
mean *scrubbed*.

"Thursday is market day," my aunt finally announced, and silently Uncle Diep unfolded himself

from his Vietnamese newspaper, took out his wallet, counted the bills stuffed in it, and lifted a Boston Red Sox baseball cap from the hook by the door.

"He goes to South Boston to buy fresh produce," Nancy explained as my aunt followed Uncle Diep to the door, spurting out a barrage of instructions in Vietnamese. "Ma's reminding him that last time we ran out of limes and cabbage—"

Nancy was interrupted by a wail from the street. "That's Luu," Vinny exclaimed.

He loped over to the window, where he groaned. "Oh, good grief, not *again*. Ma, there's trash all over the back stairs."

Peering over Vinny's shoulder, I caught a glimpse of fruit rinds, broken glass, paper, and rotting vegetables sliming the stairs Nancy and I'd sat on last night. Luu was shaking her head and wailing, *"Xau, xau."*

"Of course it's bad. Foolish woman!" Lien shoved me aside to stand, hands on hips, at the window. "Clean it up," she shouted in English and then followed this with a string of Vietnamese. "If there is mess on back stairs," she said to us, "mess must be in front of restaurant, too. I go help Luu. Nguyen, Vinh, Mai—take broom and shovel and bucket of water and go in front. Pham—"

But Pham, muttering that he had an early class, was already making tracks toward his room. Vinny started to edge off, too. "I have to go to summer school, Ma," he protested.

"You don't have to go summer school till nine-thirty. Plenty time to help clean now," Lien commanded. "Go in front with others."

The front was a disaster area. Not content with strewing the contents of somebody's trash can all over the sidewalk, someone had smeared the restaurant's windows with what looked and smelled like rotten eggs.

"Yuk," Nancy exploded as she hosed the windows down. "Gross! Damn that Sammy, I hope he drops dead."

51

"He's done this before?" I asked as I shoveled stuff into garbage bags and tried to ignore the smell. "Why don't you call the police?"

"Oh, sure," Vinny said bitterly. "Like they'd do anything. They haven't even caught the creeps who torched Ly's last month. And you think they did anything last week, when our front window got smashed?"

"A couple of uniforms came over and wanted to know if we had proof that the Pearls were involved," Nancy cut in. "And while the cops were here taking notes, Sammy Vuong and his jerky friends were standing across the street, laughing."

Furiously, she sprayed water over the sidewalk. "I *told* Ma last night, but does she listen? It'll go on and get worse unless we wise up and pay them protection money—like the Jade Palace people do."

I followed her gaze down Springvale Street to the Chinese restaurant with its bright green roof. It looked spanking clean and successful. A woman in a print blouse and black pants was sweeping in front, and as I watched, she shaded her eyes against the sun to look our way.

"She's probably laughing at us," Nancy muttered. "Well, why shouldn't she? Since the Jade Palace opened up, we've lost more than half our regulars."

Cousin Luu came plodding around the house hefting a bucket and a broom, and set to work helping us sweep. She kept shaking her head and muttering, "*Xau, xau*—bad, bad," under her breath.

"I've got to get going to school," Vinny said.

He broke off and gave this massive yawn. "How long did you play Deathwatch?" I asked, and he shrugged. "Watch it, or you'll get Nintendo thumb, like David."

Vinny wanted to know who David was. While I was explaining, I recalled that when I'd finally phoned Serena yesterday, David—he was home from the hospital and bored out of his skull—had hogged the phone for five minutes telling me that he'd got-

52

ten to level fifteen in his latest video game and that he itched like crazy underneath his cast.

"Bummer," Vinny sympathized. "I broke my arm one time playing soccer. Right before the kite contest, too."

He then stopped sweeping to explain that a bunch of Vietnamese kids in the neighborhood made kites and flew them near the reservoir at Chestnut Hill on Labor Day weekend.

"Like they used to in Vietnam—you know?" Vinny's eyes lit up as he added, "And you can only fly a kite you build yourself. I won last year—with that kite."

He nodded to the red and gold butterfly that hung on the restaurant wall. "You *made* that?" I gasped. "That is awesome." Vinny pinkened with pleasure. Then he added that if I liked, he'd take me kite-flying one day.

That was all the time we had to talk, because Lien came outside to see how the mop-up crew was doing. It was time, she said, to quit fooling around and get our hands into some real work.

Nancy was right—Lien was made of steel. Vinny escaped to summer school, but she kept the rest of us washing and scraping until she was satisfied. Then, after we'd cleaned to her specifications, we trooped inside to prepare Grandma Bach Thi's spring rolls.

Lien and Luu dealt with making the delicate wrappers for the rolls, but Nancy and I were the designated choppers. Under Lien's direction ("Too big— you cut too big! Ha? We not making food for elephants,") I minced pounds of shrimps, gallons of cabbage, bowls of mushrooms and scallions. I'd eaten spring rolls before—liked them even—but by the time Lien announced that we were now ready for the lunch crowd, all that had changed and I knew I'd never feel friendly toward spring rolls again.

Unfortunately, no real crowd appeared. The same went for the dinner shift, even though I recognized

53

at least one satisfied customer—the elderly man I'd seen snoozing in his chair yesterday. Apparently not all regulars had deserted the Spring Restaurant.

Once again Nancy took orders and waited tables, I washed and set up, and Vinny ran trays of food and dishes back and forth from the kitchen. Pham, looking as if he's sucked on lemons, peered through the swinging doors into the restaurant and saw me scrubbing down one of the booths.

"You still slaving away?" he asked in his snide, nasal way.

"Looks like it," I said.

"I bet Iowa never looked so good," he said.

I glanced over to where Lien, smiling like she never smiled for us, walked around the little restaurant talking and bowing and shaking hands, welcoming new customers, pausing to ask about their families and businesses. One thing I had to say about my aunt—she was a good businesswoman.

"This place isn't doing so good," Pham went on as if he were pleased about it. "The Jade Palace has specials every night, and their prices are cheaper. Plus the restaurant is a lot bigger and fancier. Naturally the people go there."

"How can they charge so little?" I asked.

"They don't pay their help," Pham said as if that explained everything. When I looked at him, puzzled, he snorted disgust at my ignorance and turned his back.

My aunt wasn't paying me, either, and I was sure she wasn't paying her kids. Luu was getting starvation wages, and no doubt Pham was working for his board, keep, and education. Of us all, I thought sourly, Pham was getting the best deal—for now. When he was a big lawyer, he'd probably be expected to help others in the family.

Lien pushed past me, touched a spot I'd missed, and clicked her tongue. "You better do again," she commented.

As I went back to work, I reminded myself that I

was accomplishing half of what I'd come to Boston to do. I was already getting a hands-on lesson on how Asian families lived. Now all I had to do was learn about my own Vietnamese roots.

That night after work I tried to talk to Lien about Mai Hongvan, but she brushed me off. "Have to do day's accounts," she told me. "Talk later."

But the opportunity to have that talk never seemed to come. At first I'd had the delusion that we had the weekend off, but Saturday and Sunday were apparently the busiest days of the week. On Saturday we did a lot of takeout business, and on Sunday Diep cooked up some kind of Vietnamese brunch that actually packed them in.

"Lots of people like Diep's cooking," Lien boasted, her gaunt cheeks flushed with pleasure. "He make good *tom kho tau* and *bo nuong kim tien*, you bet. And Grandma Bach Thi's spring rolls are best in Boston. People always want recipe, but I never give."

She took a deep, appreciative whiff, but I nearly gagged. I'd watched my uncle cook so much Vietnamese food that even though his beef rolls stuffed with bitter melon and fried prawns were a hit with the customers, they were the last things I ever wanted to eat. In fact, what I really craved was a good burger and lots of fries.

Then, unexpectedly, there was a reprieve. On Monday morning at breakfast, Nancy announced, "It's my day to go to the center. I'm leaving at one."

Uncle Diep didn't take his eyes off the Vietnamese newspaper he was reading. Pham had his nose buried in a textbook and Vinny just kept eating his Cheerios. Aunt Lien reared up her head and demanded, "Why you have to go so early?"

"Because on Thursday we picked up Mai at the airport," my cousin pointed out. "I couldn't go, remember? I promised Dr. Sayel I'd try to be there early this week."

My aunt's lips folded in a straight line. "One o'clock

is too early. Middle of lunch," she decreed. "Jade Palace closed Monday, so we will have plenty customers."

"Ma," Nancy said, "I promised the doctor I'd come early."

It seemed as though a struggle was going on in my aunt's face. Finally, she gave an unhappy little nod. "You promise to go, you must go. It's your duty to doctor."

Seeing that I was in the dark, Nancy explained that she volunteered two afternoons a week at a place called the Sayel Center. "Dr. Sayel started it back in the seventies." She paused and asked brightly, "Hey, want to come with me?"

"No," said Lien.

A shaft of rebellion stirred. I mean, what the heck, I wasn't her *slave*. I'd been working since I arrived in Boston, and for sure I had some free time coming.

"I'd like to go to the Sayel Center with Nancy," I said. Lien scowled at me. She was waiting for me to back down, but I recalled the Houston bylaw—square up to trouble, don't run from it—and met her unwinking gaze. "I really would like to go," I repeated.

"We'll be back by six," Nancy added. She turned to me and explained, really serious, "Dr. Sayel started the center to help poor people get medical help. Now it does a lot more—offers legal advice, family counseling, stuff like that. Judy Reubins, the lady who is in charge of the outreach program, needs volunteers to help her."

She broke off to level a sweet smile at Lien. "Dr. Sayel helped us out when we first came to this country. Didn't she, Ma?"

Lien muttered under her breath.

"Back then we were sponsored by a church." Nancy turned back to me, her face looking earnest and sincere until she lowered her eyelid in a wink. "We didn't have any money the winter I came down with pneumonia. Ma took me to Dr. Sayel, and she treated me for free."

She stopped a beat to let this all sink in and then

added, "That's why I volunteer at the Sayel Center—to pay back our debt to the doctor."

I was no dummy. "My mom always says people have to pay their debts," I agreed.

Lien looked from me to Nancy. She knew that we were putting something over on her, but she didn't know what to do about it.

After a moment she nodded grudgingly. "Be back before six," she rapped out, and then started chewing Pham out for something in Vietnamese.

Freedom! It'd never tasted so sweet as when, at one o'clock that afternoon, Nancy and I left the Spring Restaurant behind and walked up Springvale Street. It was a fine July day, already shimmery with heat, but the green-leafed trees gave us shade until we reached the corner of Harvard and Springvale. Here a small, fat, gray dust-mop of a dog charged at us, growling and snapping.

"Back off, Peterbilt," Nancy shouted. "Tommy—get this mutt off me."

The skinny Vietnamese boy I'd seen the first day I'd landed in Boston—Vinny's friend, Tommy Vuong—came trotting to the door of the Megabytes store. He was homely and as gangly as Vinny, but he was quick on his feet. Scooping up the dog, he said, "Sorry about that. I'd like to keep him leashed, but Mr. Singh thinks it'd be cruel."

"Mr. Singh's going to be sued one day when his hound bites someone," Nancy warned, and he gave us an apologetic smile. Unliked his elder brother, Tommy seemed friendly.

"You must be Mai," he said to me. "Vinny was telling me about you. You guys not working at the restaurant today, Nancy?"

"No, we're off," we both said at the same time, and then we stopped to grin each other. "Yes!" Nancy exclaimed.

We did high-fives and burst out laughing. "That look on Aunt Lien's face," I chortled. "It was priceless."

"She'll find some other way to make our lives miserable," Nancy assured me as we waved good-bye to Tommy and headed up Harvard Avenue. "She'll take it out of our hides. Tomorrow we'll work, work, work, till we drop."

Nancy puffed her cheeks in frustration. "I can understand it in a way—I mean, Ma and Papa left everything they owned in Vietnam and nearly died to get here, so they want to make good—but it kills me because Ma's so damned pigheaded about everything. It's her way or the highway."

I didn't say anything. "It's not like you thought it would be, is it?" I shook my head. "What *did* you expect, anyway?" Nancy then asked. "I mean, why did you suddenly decide to come?"

I hesitated, not sure whether I wanted to talk about Billy Lintell. "My folks always talked about my Vietnamese roots," I hedged. "I wanted to know more about that part of me."

"You won't get anything out of Ma," Nancy warned. "She doesn't like talking about the bad old days. Mr. Vuong, now, will go on and on."

Sammy and Tommy's dad had left Vietnam with the Tranhs. "He must have known Mai Hongvan," I murmured.

Nancy gave me a funny look. "Why do you always call her Mai Hongvan?" she wanted to know. "Isn't she your mother?"

"My *birth* mother," I corrected her. "My adopted folks are my mom and dad."

"It's confusing," Nancy said. Then, as we reached Brighton Avenue and climbed aboard a green and white streetcar headed for Union Square, she added, "Anyway, Mr. Vuong will definitely tell you a lot more than Ma ever will. She feels that Aunt Mai was a disgrace. I mean, running around with GIs and stuff like that."

I wondered if I should feel defensive, but I didn't. I mean, how could I feel for someone I didn't know? And the truth of it was that I knew no more about Mai Hongvan than I did before coming to Boston.

And I had Lien to thank. As we rattled along, I saw a sign that proclaimed DO A RANDOM ACT OF KINDNESS and wondered if, in spite of the way she helped people in her family, Lien was really a kind person. If she was, you couldn't prove it by me. She hadn't even called me by my name except to introduce me to someone.

Uneasy thoughts about my blood aunt kept me company till we got off at Union Square. Here groups of kids, hanging out or listening to loud rap and hip-hop music, watched us turn down Garvin Road, and a couple of guys in long white and red T-shirts whistled suggestively.

"Ignore them," Nancy sniffed. "Stupid CKs! Just keep walking."

Garvin Road was long, winding, and lined with older brick and wooden houses. It was also what my social studies teacher back in Serena would call an ethnically mixed neighborhood. I saw African American women pushing strollers and an old Asian man walking a dog. I heard Spanish music coming from one house, reggae from another, and boom-box rock coming from some stairs where a bunch of young black guys, baseball caps sitting backward on their heads, were sitting and drinking beer.

Halfway down this street was the Sayel Center. This was a homely two-story brick and wooden house ringed by neatly clipped bushes and fronted by a garden my mom would have killed for. I'd never seen so many flowers and so many colors in one place before: bloodred cannas, pink geraniums, purplish dahlias, roses, shasta daisies, and hollyhock mingled with marigolds and petunias in beds, in pots, and in baskets that hung from the front porch.

Nancy told me that the garden was the work of Hector Gonsalves. "He's an old guy who used to work for the center as a gardener. He's too old and too arthritic to do much now, but he still keeps the place looking nice."

She led the way up to the porch and through a

glass and wooden door into a foyer where a bulletin board announced that Family Group met at six on Wednesdays in Judy's room and that Legal Council would be held on Fridays at six-thirty. Past the bulletin board was a fair-size waiting room painted a pale blue. A group of people were sitting and reading, others were hanging around a coffee machine, and some toddlers were playing in a corner. One little girl was lying flat on her back on the dark blue indoor-outdoor carpeting and sucking on a bottle.

"Nancy! It's good to see you, honey. Who's your friend?"

A plump African American woman with harlequin glasses was waving to us from a little alcove marked Reception. Nancy introduced me, adding, "My cousin came all the way from Iowa to help out at the center, Mrs. Menzies."

The woman with the glasses said, now, wasn't that sweet of me. "Judy will be delighted to see both of you girls," she added. "Maria's out with the stomach flu, and she has all those circulars to stuff."

She was interrupted by an awful yell from somewhere inside the clinic. I tensed, ready to run, but nobody else seemed to be worried. The kids continued to play and their mothers just sat.

"Mr. Belrose's ingrown toenails," Mrs. Menzies sighed. "He *will* keep cutting his nails the wrong way. Doctor's a saint to put up with him."

Steering me around Mrs. Menzies's desk, Nancy led me down a corridor, past the door from which loud groans were now coming, and up to an office marked JUDY REUBINS, ADVOCATE.

Inside, talking on the phone, was a short, chunky blond woman wearing a white poet's blouse, a necklace of blue beads, denim skirt, and sneakers. "Remember that Leila's been out of work and on the streets for several months," she was saying. "We'll have to get her used to her new community in stages."

She saw us, waved, mouthed a "hi," and pointed to a full basket on her desk. I saw that it was loaded with addressed envelopes and circulars as Nancy carried it over to a card table set up near the desk.

"We stuff the circulars in the envelopes," she explained. "Ta-daa! The excitement for the day."

"What excitement am I missing?" Judy asked. She had a cheerful but calm voice, a way of speaking that was as relaxing as the smile with which she thanked me for coming to help.

"Boy, do we need you, Mai," she said. "Getting Leila Protney settled in a halfway house took all morning, so I'm behind on everything. Want a cup of coffee before we plunge in, girls?"

"She's always on the run," Nancy commented as Judy trotted out of the office. "If she's not with her clients or in her meetings or with the Family Group, she's busy thinking up new ways of raising money so's to keep the center going—"

Nancy broke off and glanced at her watch. "Oh, dammit—look at the time. I don't believe what I just did."

I asked her what she'd done and Nancy told me that she'd forgotten to run an incredibly important errand. "I meant to do it before we came to the center, but we got to talking and I totally forgot," she moaned. "Listen, Mai, could you cover for me while I go and take care of it right now?"

I said, sure, no problem, and even before the words were out of my mouth, Nancy was gone. Whatever she'd forgotten to do, I thought, had to be really important for her to move so fast.

There were footsteps in the hall behind me. Assuming that it was Judy with the coffee, I didn't turn my head until a shy male voice said, "*Hola, Señora* Judy Reubins?"

Two people were standing just inside Judy's office. One of them was a little, thin, gray-haired old man dressed in faded but neat blue jeans and a white shirt with a bandanna around his throat. He leaned on a cane with one hand and had the other arm draped across the shoulders of the blond-headed boy with him.

The old man was about five feet two. His helper, who looked to be about my age, had to be close to six feet, which meant he had to scrunch down and walk bent-kneed. On top of this, he was hefting a brown grocery bag that looked full to the brim and pretty heavy.

"Hi," the tall boy said to me. "Is Judy around?"

I said she'd just left the office. "In that case, permit us to leave these with you," said the little old man. He had a heavy accent, but he spoke each word so carefully in his soft voice that I understood everything he said. "Jon, kind friend, if you will put the sack down there—"

The blond boy set the bag down by Judy's desk. As he did so, a humongous tomato rolled out and landed at my feet.

"Fruits of the soil, señorita." When he smiled, the old man's face creased like brown parchment. "Pardon my rudeness—I am Hector Cruz Gonsalves, at your service."

I introduced myself, and he bobbed this funny little bow. "Señorita Mai, a pleasure to meet you. This is my friend Jon Delaney, on whose strong arm I rely. He—ah, but forgive me, here is Señor Nate," he added as a big, broad-chested African American man appeared in the hall. "Is the doctor ready for me, amigo?"

The blond boy, Jon Delaney, waved at me as they left, and a second later Judy came in with three cups of coffee.

"Ah-ha," she said when she saw the tomatoes. "Hector strikes again." She set down the coffees, picked up a tomato, and took an appreciative whiff. "So early in the season, too. The Family Group will love these."

"He really is quite a gardener," I said, "My mom has a vegetable garden, too, but her tomatoes never looked like this."

Judy came over to help me fold and stuff the last of the circulars. "Hiring Hector to landscape the center's front yard was the smartest thing we ever did."

She told me that she'd gotten to know Mr.

Gonsalves ten years ago in Cambridge, while she was involved in helping refugees from El Salvador.

"Hector had been beaten and tortured by government-backed soldiers before he managed to escape," she said, "but there was no bitterness in him—he was the gentlest soul—and we hit it off right away. I helped him find work and a place to live, and Dr. Sayel and I coached him for his citizenship exam. He can barely walk now because of bad arthritis, but he still spends as much time as he can in his garden. Jon helps whenever he can."

I gathered that the blond boy was another volunteer, and Judy said that he was the second-generation Delaney on the job.

"We hang on to our people," she added. "Our R.N., Nate Johnson, used to be one of our clients back in the early eighties. And there's Nancy's family, which—by the way, where *is* Nancy?"

I explained, and Judy praised me for doing a really good job on my own. "There goes my phone," she added. "Would you mind taking this batch of envelopes out to the front and giving them to Mrs. M. to mail?"

As I was walking down the hall I saw the front door open and in came a young Asian woman in print shirt and dark, baggy pants. She was holding a baby tightly against her chest and looked scared to death.

Mrs. Menzies said, "Hello," which made the newcomer look even more frightened. With her pale skin and tied-back hair, she looked like a terrified rabbit, and her voice shook as she said something I couldn't understand.

"I'm sorry, dear, I don't speak your language," Mrs. Menzies protested. "Is your baby sick?"

Just then the newcomer spotted me. Her eyes lit up, and she ran toward me, grabbed my arm, and pushed her baby toward me, all the time babbling in her unknown language.

"Lan," she wailed, and when I stared at her, she shook my arm, frantically. *"Wa!"* she cried.

And then she burst into tears.

63

Chapter Five

Mrs. Menzies came running out of her reception area. "Get Dr. Sayel," she directed, but the baby's mother clung to me even tighter and held me back.

"What's happening here?"

A tall, gray-haired woman in doctor's whites was striding toward us. Behind her came the big nurse, Nate. At the sight of them, the baby's mother burst into a stream of words. "Slow down," the doctor said, and followed this with a string of unfamiliar words.

Whatever she was saying, it sounded crisp and authoritative, and the mother let go of me. But as she held her child toward the doctor, the baby stiffened and then went limp. Its mouth slackened, its eyes rolled up.

Dr. Sayel scooped the baby out of its mother's arms and took off down the hallway. "Nate," she called over her shoulder, "phenobarbital—stat!"

The mother started to follow, but her legs seemed to give out from under her. Wailing and sobbing, she fell down onto her knees and knocked her head on the floor.

"Oh, my Lord," breathed Mrs. Menzies. "Talk to her, Mai. She seems to trust you."

How could I talk to her when I didn't speak a word of her language? Feeling like crying myself, I knelt down and patted the woman's back. "It's going to be all right," I gabbled.

"Lan," moaned the poor woman. Then she reared up, grabbed my hands, and burst into passionate, pleading words.

"I wish I knew what you're saying," I told her. She was younger than I'd thought at first, and so pale that the red of her swollen eyes was the only color in her face. She looked so desperate and scared that I had to do *something*, so I put my arms around her and rocked her the way Mom used to rock Liz and me when we were kids.

"It's going to be okay, really," I crooned. "The doctor's taking care of your baby—"

Just then there was the sound of an infant crying from down the hall. Pushing away from me, the mother jumped to her feet and took off in the direction of that cry. I caught up to her at the door of the consulting room in time to see the baby lying on the consulting table without a stitch on. She had ice under her neck and in her armpits, and Nate, his big hands gentle, was sponging her down with water and crooning to her while the doctor measured out medicine.

The mother ran toward her child. "Is the baby okay?" I asked Nate.

He nodded. "Her temp probably caused the seizure—she was running close to a hundred and six. Don't worry, she's doing good now. Dr. S. has everything under control."

Dr. Sayel was talking to the mother in her own language. Nate gave me another nod and a grin—thanks, Mai, we can manage without you now. I started to leave the room and then glanced back. The mother was bending over her baby, patting it, kissing its small hands, and whispering to it. Watching her brought a king-size lump into my throat, so I got out of there fast.

I met Judy hovering in the hall and told her what happened. She said, "Bet you didn't think you'd have such a busy first day here," then added that she had to leave to see a patient at Brighton Memorial Hospital and that I was to start addressing a stack of envelopes to major corporations and foundations in the area.

"We're looking for sponsors for the Thanksgiving concert—it's our biggest fund-raiser," she explained. "Use your fanciest handwriting, okay? Nancy can help you when she comes in."

Where had that girl gone? I wondered as I sat down at Judy's desk and started copying addresses from a sheet of paper. I was into my fifth envelope when I heard decisive footsteps in the hall and Dr. Sayel walked in.

"Mai Houston, isn't it?" When I said it was, she said, "I wanted to come and thank you for helping us back there."

I shook her cool, long-fingered hand and asked, how was the baby? The doctor said the fever was coming down. "She had a flaming red throat," she went on. "I've taken a culture, but I'd bet my right arm that it's strep."

"Will she be okay?" I asked.

"You'd better believe it," Dr. Sayel replied briskly. "I'm keeping Baby Orchid under observation, and if she's no better by this evening, I'll have her taken to Children's." She frowned. "I wish my Chinese were better. Half the time I don't think Big Orchid understood me."

I said it was funny that both mother and child had the same name. "I don't know that for sure. The baby's name is Lan—orchid—and since the mother wouldn't give her name, Big Orchid she will have to be till further notice."

The doctor's high-cheekboned face softened into a smile. All the features under her mane of silver hair were bold: dark line of eyebrows, strong, slightly crooked nose, and decisive mouth. Dr. Sayel almost looked forbidding—except for the humor in her wide-spaced gray eyes.

"You kept your cool and thought on your feet," she went on. "Also, Mrs. M. says you showed a lot of savvy when Big Orchid fell apart. I like to see that in my crew."

She made it sound as if my coming back to work

at the center was a given, but I didn't mind. I liked her. Every move the doctor made was swift and precise, and she seemed to burn with energy. I could definitely understand why even Lien Van Tranh had a healthy respect for this lady.

I went back to writing out addresses until five o'clock, when I knew I couldn't wait for Nancy any longer. If I didn't get myself back to the Spring Restaurant, my aunt would have a fit. So I told Mrs. Menzies good-bye, told Nate that I hoped that Baby Orchid would be okay, and left the clinic.

Once outside, I started walking toward Union Square. Perhaps because it was later in the day, there seemed to be fewer people strolling down Garvin Road. Still, I hadn't gone halfway up the long, winding road to the square before I heard footsteps and voices behind me.

Glancing over my shoulder, I saw several guys. They all wore baggy pants that were way too long for them, T-shirts stenciled with a drawn sword dripping blood, and black baseball caps turned backward. They strode along in their high-tops as if they owned the street.

"Hey, sweet-cheeks, whatchyu doin' tonight?" one of them called. Then he whistled softly, and all the others did, too.

I walked more quickly, and male laughter and more whistles followed me. The footsteps behind me grew louder and there were kissing sounds. "She don't like you, Squint," someone snickered.

I was getting really scared, but I kept walking. I told myself that I'd soon be at Union Square, reminded myself that nothing could happen to me in broad daylight.

"Now, baby, be nice," another mocking voice called, and my flesh crawled. There was more laughter and then—silence. That was the worst of all. All I could hear in this awful stillness were my own breathing and the footsteps. Footsteps moving faster, *faster*—catching up with me.

Remembering those skinheads, remembering Billy Lintell, I wondered what they were going to do with me. Spray-paint me red, or— *Don't run,* I warned myself. *Don't show them you're scared.*

I caught a glimpse of movement out of the corner of my eye and felt dry-mouthed fear. "Hey, wait up," a familiar voice said.

I nearly died with relief as the blond boy from the center, Jon Delaney, hopped off the bike he was riding and fell into step next to me. "Are you training for the marathon?" he wondered.

As he spoke, the guys who'd been following me strutted past us, laughing as if at some big joke. Jon was saying, "Mrs. Menzies was afraid you'd get lost on your way to Union Square."

"Were—were you with Mr. Gonsalves all this time?" I asked. My voice wasn't too steady, and Jon looked sideways at me.

"You okay?" he asked. "Did those CKs hassle you?"

I asked him who the CKs were and Jon said they were a gang—one of many in Boston. "In some parts of the city there's a gang fighting to control turf on every block," he explained. "They don't think twice about blowing someone away, either. We're talking about some really twisted dudes."

I felt a cold knot forming in my stomach. "Why don't the police arrest them?"

"They do, but most times the gang members go right back on the streets." Jon added, "This area has been pretty quiet till recently, but then the CKs and Pearls moved in. According to Nate Johnson, though, the gangs might just kill each other over business."

Apparently both the Pearls and the CKs were heavy into extortion and were warring for control of key streets. "There've been suspicious fires and broken windows and stuff. Cops think that the Pearls are behind a lot of home invasions, too, but so far they can't prove it, Nate says."

I asked how the R.N. at the Sayel Center came to know so much about gangs, and Jon said that Nate had run with a gang before getting involved with Dr. Sayel and the center.

"Gang members walk into the center all the time," he added. "A couple of weeks ago, some guy walked in with a knife still sticking through his shoulder."

"Oh, gross," I gasped. "What'd you do?"

"Panic." Jon's grin started slowly at the corners of his mouth and then spread all over his face and into his eyes. Even the freckles on his nose seemed to be laughing. "I mean, there he was, like Rambo, bleeding all over the floor. Mrs. Menzies had a fit, especially since Nate was out sick, but Doc Sayel was really cool. I've never seen *anything* faze her."

After what had happened today, I could believe it. As I was telling Jon about the Orchids, I found myself wondering how my mom would have coped with a Chinese-speaking mother and a convulsing baby. But then, Boston seemed a million light-years away from Serena. . . .

"Maybe not," Jon said, and I realized I'd spoken my last thought out loud. "Wherever they come from, people are people—quote, unquote, courtesy of Hector Cruz Gonsalves. Uh—where *is* Serena, anyway?"

I told him, and he went, "Iowa, huh? And your last name's Houston?"

Something inside me tightened. *Now he's going to ask the big question,* the familiar voice in my mind whispered, and I readied myself for either (a) "So, I guess you're adopted?" or (b) "Is your mother or your father Asian?" or even (c) "How come an Asian girl has a name like Houston?"

"With a name like Houston, you should live in Texas," Jon was saying.

I stared at him, and then burst out laughing. "That's awful," I groaned.

"Hey, you're hurting my feelings." By now we had reached Union Square and a green and white street-car was rattling into view. "You sure you can get home okay?" When I nodded, he added, "Okay, Iowa, see you Thursday."

As I watched Jon's tall, waving figure grow smaller, I found myself grinning like a fool. Why had I laughed at such a corny joke? With a name like Houston—oh, *please*. It was the kind of dumb thing that would have cracked David up.

And, speaking of the brat, I realized that I hadn't heard from my family since I'd reached Boston. Even when Liz and I were at camp, Mom used to write us twice a week and call us, too. Strange—until I remembered that before I left I'd insisted that she cut me some slack, that I needed my space when I was with the Tranhs. Mom had promised me not to interfere in any way.

The residue of good feeling slid away as I remembered the hurt in Mom's voice and the look in her eyes when she gave me that promise. No, I thought, it really wasn't so surprising that I hadn't heard from Serena.

While munching over this thought, I got confused and missed getting off at Harvard Avenue. It was cutting six when I reached the restaurant, where I found the kitchen crew working double-time. Uncle Diep hardly acknowledged my arrival, and Pham just gave me a dirty look, but Vinny asked me where did I get off, coming home so late?

My younger cousin looked beat, and his lower lip was twisted down so that he almost looked like Pham. "What's with you?" I demanded.

"You get to go where you want while I end up by getting yelled at," Vinny growled. "I'm sick of it. Go here, do this, carry this, work, work, work or Gian can't make it over here. I wish Gian would just drop dead."

As he hefted a laden tray through the swinging doors, Nancy walked into the kitchen. "Boy, you run fast," she said to me. "Didn't you hear me yelling for you to wait up?"

She acted as if we'd come home from the center to-

70

gether. "Where did you go this afternoon?" I demanded, and she pinched my arm hard.

"Not so loud," she warned. "They can hear you."

She pushed me through the swinging doors into the restaurant just as a customer came in. He was one of the regulars—the old guy I'd seen on my first day in Boston.

"Hi, Mr. Vuong," Nancy said, all smiles and charm. "You're early tonight. Will you have the usual?"

I looked curiously at Sammy and Tommy Vuong's father. Mr. Vuong had the long, wrinkled neck of a tortoise and he had the habit of looking around him apprehensively before he spoke. "I'm in big hurry tonight, Nguyen," he said in a low, raspy voice. "Just bring me meat and noodles and *tra*."

"Sure, Mr. Vuong." Nancy nudged me and whispered, "He's the one to ask about, *you* know." I hesitated, and Nancy gave me another little push. "Lookit—he's staring at you. Get over there and talk to him before Ma comes out and sees you."

Uncertainly, I walked over to Mr. Vuong's table. He was still staring at me. "What is your name?" he demanded. I told him and he let out a long breath like a hiss. "I thought so. Mai Hongvan's daughter. Sure."

My heart did a flutter. Sitting down in the chair across from him, I asked, "You knew me right away, Mr. Vuong?"

He bobbed his head up and down several times. "Sure," he said. "My son Tommy tell me Vinh's cousin was coming Boston."

"Aunt Lien said you came out of Vietnam with her and Mai Hongvan," I ventured.

"*Co tyu*—certainly. We all go Hong Kong on that boat," Mr. Vuong sighed. "Was too many people, no food, bad storms. Man who ran boat, he care only about taking our money. All we prayed for was to get away."

He steepled his hands together as if praying now. "We were hungry and thirsty. First day on sea comes

71

a bad storm and many of us were very sick. Very afraid. Lien's baby girl is very sick. Her older boy, he die of the fever."

I actually felt the hairs stand up on the back of my neck. "Lien had a son who d-died?" I stammered.

"Sure. His name Khi. Six year old when he die." Mr. Vuong gulped hard and began rubbing his hands together. "Other kids die, too, and one old man die. He carried off by wave during storm."

He broke off, chewing his lower lip, and I reminded myself that I'd heard these awful stories before. My mom had made all us kids read about the ordeal endured by the Vietnamese boat people. "Reality check," she'd called it. But though accounts of storms and starvation and death were terrible, we'd read about them while we were well fed and safe in Serena.

But now here I was, sitting across from Mr. Vuong, who was listing really gruesome events in a monotonous, almost emotionless voice.

"Was—was Mai Hongvan sick, too?" I whispered.

"No. She get sick later, after we reach camp in Hong Kong." Mr. Vuong squinted down at his thick, brown, steepled fingers. "She become very sick from having baby."

From having *me*, he meant. Out of the corner of my eye I saw Lien framed in the swinging doorway. I didn't have much time. Urgently, I asked, "Do I look like her?"

"No," he said flat out. "Her skin was more golden, eyes were different. You are big and tall because not pure-blooded Vietnamese." Sudden, unexpected pain flooded his eyes. "Mai too much pretty. Had long black hair, walked like graceful bird. She liked flowers, was always singing—"

"Hey, Pops."

Sammy Vuong had walked in the restaurant door. His long black hair was slicked back in a ponytail, and he wore a white T-shirt and tight black jeans. As he sauntered toward us, his arrogant dark eyes were glued to his dad.

Mr. Vuong seemed to shrivel even more into himself. He spoke in Vietnamese, and Sammy said, "Never mind that crap. I told you not to come in here no more."

Red mottled all over the old man's face. He slapped his hand on the table and shouted, "You not tell me what to do!"

Sammy leaned down, planted his fists on the table, and glared down at his father. "I didn't hear you say that, old man," he said. Then he spat something out in Vietnamese.

Mr. Vuong went even redder. He opened his mouth, but nothing came out. "You go on home, old man," Sammy Vuong went on. "You want to eat, you go to the Jade Palace, understand?"

Mr. Vuong said nothing. He did nothing. He just sat where he was. Sammy reached over and gave the old man a light tap on top of his head. From what Mom had made me read about Vietnamese customs, I knew that this was an insult.

Sammy waited for his father to do something. When Mr. Vuong didn't react, he shrugged, gave Lien, who was glaring at him, a mocking salute, then turned to me. "See you around, *con lai*."

As he swaggered outside, I saw that several other guys, all more or less dressed like Sammy and wearing the black pearl in one ear, were waiting. They exchanged some kind of twisting handshake before walking away.

"Ah, *lay chua, lay chua!*" Mr. Vuong had clasped his hands together. He now lowered his head and started praying. Tears were running down his face, but he didn't even wipe them away. I felt sick for him.

There was nothing to do but leave him to his misery. At least, I consoled myself as I walked away, now I knew that Mai Hongvan had been pretty, had walked softly and gracefully. I knew that she'd liked

73

singing and flowers. And, just as Lien had said, I looked nothing like her.

I still couldn't picture her. It was as if my birth mother and everything about her were hidden behind a curtain. When the curtain fluttered in the wind, I could see a little of what lay behind, but only a little. Not nearly enough.

It was, I resolved, time to have a talk with Lien.

"Why were you talking to crazy old Mr. Vuong?" Lien demanded. "I don't like you bothering customers."

It was eleven-thirty and the end of the workday, and the others had gone to bed. I'd stayed behind while Lien did the accounts because I was determined to ask her about Mai Hongvan, but with the first words out of my mouth, she'd gone on the offensive.

"He didn't sound crazy," I protested. "He told me about the time when you all left Vietnam for Hong Kong."

"Mr. Vuong is an old turtle," my aunt said contemptuously. She was sitting by the cash register, her forehead furrowed, her mouth tighter than usual. "He spoil his sons. Give them everything they want. Give, give, give! He let that bad boy, Sammy, show disrespect, even hit him on head! I see, cannot believe."

She paused to shake her head. Her face was half in shadow, but I could tell she was angry as she added, "All old turtle can do is pray to Buddha. Besides, his memory not too good."

"Mr. Vuong's memory seemed plenty good," I persisted. "He told me about the leaky boat and—and about people dying at sea." Lien's already hard mouth tightened further. "Is that the way it happened?"

"What else did old fool say?" I hesitated, not wanting to talk about Khi, yet wanting to know. "Old man Vuong tell you about Khi," Lien charged.

My aunt broke off, squared her shoulders, and

looked directly at me, and something in her manner reminded me of my own mom. "That boy already sick when we get on the boat. Storm brings fever. He die, we bury him at sea. Is this what you want to know?"

I felt about two inches tall. Ashamed by the expression in her eyes, I whispered, "I'm sorry."

Lien snorted. "Why? You didn't do nothing. Anyway, all this happen long ago." She started to get up, but I called her back. "What now?" she asked impatiently.

I wanted to ask more about that terrible journey, and their stay in the refugee camps, about how Mai Hongvan had died. So many questions—but from the look in her eyes, Lien wasn't going to answer any of them. "If I don't look like Mai Hongvan or any of your family, who do I look like?" I blurted out.

"How should I know?" she came back quickly, biting off those words like bullets. "My sister had many American boyfriends. Maybe you look like one of them."

Is that why you don't like me? I wanted to cry. But I didn't have the nerve. I couldn't bear to face the cold, hard light in my aunt's eyes. Supposing she said yes, that was why.

I'd been warned that this could happen. My mom had said that Lien mightn't welcome memories from the past, and she'd been right. I clenched my hands in my lap and wished I'd never come to Boston.

"I don't like talking about old days," Lien was telling me. "Then is then. Now is now. Tomorrow we have to get up early."

She got to her feet and stood over me. "You have too much time," she said impatiently. "That's why you think stupid things. My sister is dead nearly sixteen years, she is ashes now. Why you want to bring back her ghost? Our home in Vietnam smashed down, burned away. Khi is dead. All finished. What you want to know about such things for?"

"I just want to know about my roots," I muttered.

"Roots—that useless talk," accused my aunt. "You

stop thinking selfishness, stop thinking about yourself. You here now to help work and get Gian. If you not want to work anymore, you can go home anytime."

I felt as if I'd been slapped. As I listened to Lien's footsteps retreating, I wanted to cry for my dreams of finding a long-lost family in Boston.

The question was, now what? Did I call it quits and fly home to Serena? A part of me wanted to do just that and forget I ever heard of Lien Van Tranh and her sister.

Oh, sure. At the first sense of trouble, you're giving up, sneered a voice in the back of my mind. *What will they say in Serena when you crawl home like a whipped pup?*

Totally depressed, I slunk off to bed. I wished Nancy were up to talk to, but she was fast asleep, so I lay on my narrow cot thinking about what had happened today until I drifted off and dreamed that I was on a farm.

It was a big farm, the kind I'd seen just outside Serena all my life, with fields and a barn and animals. There were wildflowers everywhere, and a girl with long black hair was sitting in the middle of the field with a bundle in her arms. As I drew closer, I realized that the bundle was really a baby—Baby Orchid.

"Is she all better now?" I asked, and the mother looked up at me. But it wasn't Big Orchid—I was looking into my own face. And as I stared, the baby began to cry.

I came awake and heard not crying but laughter from the street under my window. Jumping out of bed, I looked out of the window and saw a half dozen guys standing near the street lamp. They were all in T-shirts that showed up white in the darkness, and the words that floated up toward me in the darkness were Vietnamese.

The Pearls—my heart bumped. They'd come to spread more garbage on the steps, or worse. So far, though, they didn't seem to be doing much except talking and smoking.

I was about to go wake Lien and Diep when a police siren wailed nearby. At the sound, the group under my window exchanged that same twisting handshake I'd seen Sammy Vuong use with his friends and then moved quickly on down the street.

In heart-bumping silence I waited, but the Pearls didn't come back. I'd slid back into bed and was almost asleep when there was a noise on the fire escape. Next minute, there was a scrape as the window screen went up.

The Pearl gang! Sammy Vuong trying to break in! I jolted out of bed as a shadow came through the window into our room.

"Shut up, Mai—it's me," Vinny whispered.

I barely managed to swallow the scream that was building inside my throat. "Wh-what are you doing?" I babbled.

"I got locked out," he whispered. "Nancy usually leaves the dead bolt off for me, but she must have forgot, and Pham sleeps with the window locked." He sat on the windowsill and added, "Don't tell Ma."

The alarm clock read two A.M.. "Were you at Tommy's till now?" I demanded.

"We were playing Deathworld, and then a few other guys stopped by and we talked and stuff." Vinny added enthusiastically, "Man, Deathworld is some terrific game. I wish I could have it."

"Why can't you?" I asked, thinking that having that game might keep Vinny home and out of trouble. "Save your money and buy it."

"What money?" he demanded. "Ma doesn't give us a red cent." His usually cheerful voice was suddenly harsh as he added, "If it wasn't for that damned Gian, I could have gotten a real job this summer. It's not fair. I don't even know the guy, and I have to slave for him."

Remembering my own encounter with Lien, I kept quiet. Vinny was saying, "One time I did ask Ma about getting a bunch of video games, and she shot me down. Then I had to listen to her going on about

77

how lucky I was to be alive and have meals on the table and a roof over my head."

He fumed for a few seconds and then added in a furious whisper, "Ma's too cheap to even get a decent TV set—ours is so old, it goes out of focus all the time. Work, work, work, save, save, save—I mean, it's not just the dumb video games, it's like she has to control everything I do! Sometimes I think Tommy's right when he says that the only way out of this is to—"

Uncle Diep coughed down the hall from us, and Vinny tensed. A second later he was hurrying past me toward the door, and in the dim light from the street below I saw that his arm was all bloody.

"What happened?" I gasped. "Did the—did the CKs get you?"

Vinny stopped dead in his tracks and asked me, real sharp, what I was talking about and how did I know about CKs? I told him what had happened to me that afternoon, and he launched into a lecture about how to handle myself in the city.

"There are some really twisted dudes out there," he whispered, echoing Jon Delaney, "and those CKs aren't the only ones who hate Asians. You've got to stay awake, Mai. Don't look scared or worried, and always walk near the center of the road so that people can't grab you from a building or an alley. And stay the heck away from Heather and Ringe anytime, day or night."

According to Vinny, it was okay to go to the center on Garvin Road, and Park Vale Avenue was safe, too. But Heather Avenue, which ran parallel to Park Vale, and Ringe Street, which connected Park Vale and Heather, were CK territory. Asians had better keep out or else.

While he was talking, blood was dripping down his arm. "You can tell me all this later," I interrupted. "Right now I want to know what happened to your arm." He shrugged and said he'd hurt himself when he leaned up against a nail in the Vuongs' wall. "You could get lockjaw," I said. "Come on, I'll wash it and put a bandage on it."

"One visit to the center and you're a doctor?" But then he realized I meant business. "Okay, okay," he whispered. "Don't wake up the frigging house."

"Watch your mouth," I said automatically, as I would have when I was talking to David. But this was definitely not Brat Houston who followed cautiously to the bathroom and who stood dripping blood into the sink while I rummaged through the shelves trying to locate bandages and antibiotic cream.

Bandages there were, but no cream. "Use this," Vinny said, producing a little jar with dragons all over the lid. "Ma always uses this stuff when we get hurt."

I washed the cut which had definitely not been made by any nail. It wasn't jagged but clean—the kind you got from a knife. Vinny had tangled with the CKs for sure, but he didn't want anyone to know.

He winced as I cleaned the wound and smeared stuff on it. It smelled disgusting. "Have you finished?" Vinny wanted to know.

I slapped a butterfly bandage on the clean cut and then bound it up with a roll of gauze I found on the shelf. "If it bleeds through the bandage, you're going to need stitches," I warned. "Go down to the center and Dr. Sayel'll do it for you."

"I don't have to go to anyplace. This will be fine." Then he added awkwardly, "Thanks, Mai, I owe you. How about we go fly kites early one morning, huh? My new dragon kite's almost done, and I want to give it a dry run before the contest."

I said I'd like that. Then I remembered something. "Vinny, what does *con lai* mean?"

He looked surprised. "Where did you hear that?" he asked. I said from Sammy Vuong.

"I already figured out it's an insult," I went on. "Is he calling me a moose or porker, or it some kind of Vietnamese swear word, or what?"

"Not really." Vinny hesitated, looking embarrassed. Then he said, "It means half-breed."

79

Chapter Six

THURSDAY, WHEN I went with Nancy to the Sayel Center, I asked how Baby Orchid was doing. Mrs. Menzies rolled her eyes and declared that was what she'd like to know, too.

"That mother, the one Doctor calls Big Orchid, took her baby out of the center sometime after you left," she said indignantly. "Just took her right out of here when Nate's back was turned—without Doctor's say-so and without so much as a thank-you. I saw her running out of here and asked her what she thought she was doing, but she just looked at me as if she were scared to death and took off. I didn't have time to get any information out of her, so I don't know where."

Dr. Sayel was more concerned than upset. "I'd given Big Orchid some antibiotics," she told me when I caught her between patients. "Good thing, because the culture showed that the baby has strep throat. But medicine won't do any good unless Big Orchid remembers to dose her baby regularly."

"You don't think she will?"

I had to follow Dr. Sayel into her office to ask the question. It was a comfortable office, with an old rocking chair in a corner and a big desk cluttered with about a hundred photographs. More photos, mostly of kids, and crayon drawings hung on a newly whitewashed wall. A poster in bold script proclaimed TO BE ALIVE IS POWER.

"I'm not sure that Big Orchid knows about antibiotics." Dr. Sayel paused to make a notation in a file, then added, "I think she distrusts Western medicine and would much rather rely on her friendly neighborhood Chinese apothecary."

Since my dream I'd been thinking a lot about the Orchids. "Maybe that was why she was so scared that day. But why should she come to the center?"

"Maybe Chinese medicine couldn't cure her baby." The doctor looked thoughtful. "I had the feeling Big Orchid hadn't been in the country for too long. Maybe she was just frightened of a totally unfamiliar environment. Or she could be here illegally."

According to Dr. Sayel, illegal immigrants were constantly being brought into the country by unscrupulous characters who promised them jobs and good wages and then turned around and "sold" their services to local business establishments.

"Like indentured servants," she explained, "the illegals have to work off the money they owe to the person who brought them into the country. It takes the poor things years to get out of debt. And they're scared all the time. Overworked, most likely underfed, they're frightened of their bosses. But they're even more terrified that our immigration people will learn about them and send them back where they came from."

If conditions were so awful here, I pointed out, the illegals should be glad to leave. "Not if their lives back home were even worse," she countered.

I could see why Big Orchid had been so scared. "But, scared or not, she came to the center," I mused, and Dr. Sayel said, sure she did.

"Big Orchid's a mother, and mothers defend their young. Now, scoot, Mai—I have a patient to see."

All afternoon I wondered if Mai Hongvan would have defended me if she'd lived. Would she have fed me and cared for me and kissed me the way Big Orchid kissed her little girl? I didn't realize how much these thoughts shadowed everything I did until Nancy and I were heading back to the restaurant that afternoon and she said, "So, did Mr. Vuong lay

81

a heavy trip on you, or what? You've looked a million miles away all afternoon."

I told her everything, finishing off with what Mr. Vuong had told me about Lien's son, Khi. "I didn't know you had a brother," I said. "Besides Vinny, I mean."

Nancy looked somber. "Ma has a picture of Khi in her room," she said. "It's on her spirit altar. You know, the shrine that honors all the dead people in the family."

Nancy named the people that were enshrined on Lien's spirit altar: Khi, Lien's grandparents and parents, Diep's grandparents, his parents, and a brother who had been killed in the war. "Khi's photograph was taken at the house Ma and Papa lived in when they first got married," Nancy concluded. "In the village."

I asked what kind of village this was, and Nancy said, just a village. "Thatched-roof huts and farms." She grinned suddenly. "If we'd stayed in Vietnam, Vinny would've had to herd water buffalo."

"So might you."

Pretending to be insulted, Nancy tilted up her little nose. "I'd be married already. Ma was married when she was sixteen—a year and a half younger'n I am now. So I'd be an old married lady in a white shirt and black pants, feeding my husband some rice and *dis*-gusting fish sauce and gossiping with the other women—yuk!"

She didn't say what I might have been. In the quiet family scene of that faraway village, I apparently had no place. And I wasn't alone in being excluded—Mai Hongvan hadn't made it as far as the family altar.

It was depressing, to say the least, but in contrast to my own mood, Lien seemed really up that evening. She didn't once snap at us or chew Vinny out for being clumsy, and after the customers had left, she called all of us into the restaurant and told us to sit down.

"We'll have something to eat and talk," she said.

This was so totally out of character that even Pham forgot to sneer and looked as nervous as the rest of us as Luu hauled in a tray laden with tea, cups, and—you guessed it—a big plate of spring rolls, lettuce leaves, and sauce.

"What's going on, Ma?" Nancy wanted to know.

"Nothing," Lien insisted. "You all work hard, so tonight we have little food and tea together." She looked around us at the table and added formally, "Enjoy the food."

"Beware the Greeks bringing gifts," Pham muttered out of the corner of his mouth, but he didn't dare say the words loud enough for Lien to hear.

"We not having so many customer now that Jade Palace is in business," Lien then said. "Pearl bums keep dumping garbage on steps and breaking window because we don't pay them protection. Bad news all time, but today come good news. Gian Cu write to say that the government has finished processing his request to leave. Soon he'll be here."

She sounded happier than I'd ever heard her. Her eyes fairly sparkled behind her rimless glasses, and her thin mouth actually smiled as she read from the letter, first in English—I figured she was showing off how well Gian wrote in English—and then in Vietnamese for Luu's benefit. As Luu nodded and said, "Good, good," over and over, I noticed that her eyes were sad.

She was thinking of her own kids and missing them. I felt really sorry for Luu. She was such a good-natured soul that I somehow took for granted the fact that she'd just smile and say, *"Tok, tok,"*—good, good—all the time. I hadn't stopped to think that it had to be murder working hard to bring some distant cousin over when Luu would much rather have been working for her own kids.

"So the crown prince is coming," Pham was saying. He rolled a hot spring roll in a lettuce leaf, dipped it into sauce, and popping it into his mouth, began to crunch loudly.

Ignoring this sarcasm, Lien carefully folded Gian's letter. "Okay," she said, "I have this to say. We took a loan from the bank to pay for Gian to come. We took a loan to pay for his first semester at medical school. Now money has to be paid back, so we have to work hard."

Her smiled disappeared as she looked around the table. Like a general telling her troops that tough battles were up ahead, she added, "We got to work harder."

"So what else is new?" Pham swallowed his tea, stuffed another spring roll into his mouth, and got up. "I have an early class," he muttered, and slouched insolently out.

As Lien frowned after Pham, Vinny suddenly said, "Ma, when Gian gets over here and the bank loan's repaid, can I get a job?"

"You already have job," Lien pointed out.

"I mean outside the restaurant." Vinny took a deep breath and plunged in. "Tommy works at Megabytes. You know, the electronics store on the corner. He said he could get me a job."

"You too young work outside restaurant," Lien said. She acted as if this settled everything, but Vinny wouldn't give up.

"Mr. Singh, the guy who owns the store, is cool with that. Tommy just works for him part-time. And—and if I worked for Megabytes, I could buy the stuff I want at twenty percent off."

Vinny raised his hands to gesture, and his T-shirt fell back, revealing the butterfly strip I'd put on his arm. "So, when Gian comes, can I work for Mr. Singh?" he pleaded.

Uncle Diep cleared his throat as if he were going to say something. Lien said, "No."

Vinny started to protest, but my aunt cut him short. "I don't want you hanging around with

84

Tommy Vuong," she said. "You know that. His brother is a crook."

"Ma, it's not Tommy's fault that Sammy is with the Pearls. Tommy and me are friends. We always were friends, right from kindergarten, and—"

"Lots of other kids you can be friends with," Lien interrupted. "Minh Truong is nice boy. His older brother in Harvard Law School, clerking this summer for Judge Heyson in Washington, D.C." Her voice softened in respect, then sharpened again as she resumed, "You went to kindergarten with Quan Tam, too, ha? His papa is smart man, in state politics, a real bigshot! And Phong Dinh—that boy is plenty smart. Going to make something of himself, get scholarship. That one could help you with your schoolwork."

"Ma, Tommy's my *friend*." Vinny's usually cheerful face hardened as he added, "It's not fair that you hold Sammy and the Pearls against him, and it stinks that you don't let him come around here anymore, when—"

"You have summer school tomorrow," Lien cut in. "You better go to bed now, boy."

Vinny pushed away from the table so hard that his chair skittered across the floor and crashed into the wall. He walked out, banging the door behind him. Uncle Diep frowned and mumbled something in Vietnamese, but dried up when Lien looked at him.

Nancy had been nibbling on a lettuce leaf. Now she said, "Vinny works really hard, Ma. What's so bad if he wants to earn enough money to buy a few lousy video games?"

"Vinh no need video games," Lien said stubbornly. "He need work for family, he need study at school, get ahead in life. That's all he *need*."

"You can't let go, can you?" Nancy looked up, and her eyes were as stony as Lien's. "You have to be in control. You have to be the one who jerks our strings. Like this thing about Gian Cu—it was all your idea, but guess who ends up having to work like dogs?"

85

Lien slapped the table with both hands. "What talk is this?" she shouted. "You should be happy Gian is coming to America. Should be happy you helping family."

"Why should we be happy when you're so mean to your own family?" Nancy shot back. "Like it or not, this isn't the old country, Ma. Old-country rules don't mean anything here in America, and Vinny and I are Americans."

Uncle Diep stared at Nancy wide-eyed. "Nguyen," he twittered, "that not respectful thing to say. Tell Ma you're sorry."

Lien was so mad she could hardly talk. "You don't know how lucky you are," she sputtered. "Two parents working. Restaurant and house belonging to us. Some Asian family too poor to even pay rent, you know this? Some of them don't have jobs. Children have no educations. They run wild all over town and have no respect for anyone."

Nancy got to her feet and started for the door. "Nguyen!" her mother shouted. "You come here when I talk you."

Nancy whirled. "My name is Nancy," she shouted, "not Nguyen. My name is Nancy, and I'm not your slave!"

She went out then, slamming the kitchen door behind her.

After that scene Nancy and my aunt Lien didn't speak to each other. The tension that sparked from them the next morning could have set fire to the whole block, and I was never so grateful as when Judy called from the Sayel Center.

"Two of my regular volunteers have the flu, I have to be in court to help one of our clients, and it's panic time," she said. "Not only have I got these fund-raiser letters to send off *yesterday*, but the Family Group recipes are coming in."

According to Judy, another of the center's money-making projects came from a cookbook that her Family Group put together each year. "I need to type up the recipes and get them ready for the printer," she said. "Can Lien spare you girls for a couple of hours this afternoon?"

Naturally, Lien refused to let both of us go. Only one of us, she decreed, was required to fulfill our duty to the Sayel Center. Since Nancy was more experienced in restaurant work, I was sprung, and believe me, I broke all records getting out of there.

At the center, I gratefully finished addressing envelopes until Mrs. Menzies bustled in to tell me I was needed elsewhere.

"Jon Delaney just called, honey—he's been delayed at work," she said. "He's due to pick up Hector Gonsalves in ten minutes, and if Jon's not there, that stubborn old man will try to make it over here on his own." She shook her head at this folly adding, "Will you go and fetch him? He lives at 621-D Arnold—only two blocks away."

Even if I hadn't known Mr. Gonsalves's address, I'd have had no trouble finding the place. Though the brick and stone apartment building itself looked tired and dingy, 621 had a fabulous garden.

I mean, here was a *garden*. The entire area between the apartment house and the street was landscaped with flowers and flowering bushes. On the side of the building was a fenced-in area draped with blue morning glories and string beans and practically bursting with tomato plants, peppers, and cukes.

I knocked on the door of Mr. Gonsalves's basement apartment and was told to come in. The door was open, but as soon as I stepped inside 621-D, my way was blocked by a huge gray cat that arched its back and spat at me. "Hi, kitty," I said, and it yowled bloody murder and took a swipe at me.

"Bolivar, you disgrace me." Mr. Gonsalves in spanking-clean jeans, shirt, and bandanna, had tottered into the room. "Is this the way to greet a lady, wicked one?"

The cat blinked wild yellow eyes, showed evil-looking teeth in a yawn, and began to wash an enormous paw. "I apologize for Bolivar's lack of manners," Mr. Gonsalves told me, shaking hands with a grip that was surprisingly strong for such a frail person. "He is a street cat. He was half dead of battle wounds when he crawled onto my front steps a year ago."

Mr. Gonsalves bent to scatch behind the monster's chewed-up ear, and it began a growling noise that was probably its version of a purr. "Ah, yes," crooned the old man lovingly, "you are a caballero, aren't you? You are my partner."

As Bolivar rubbed his face against Mr. Gonsalves's hand, I glanced around the tiny apartment, which smelled of coffee and flowers. There was a small kitchen off one side of the hall, and on the other was the living room. Here, under lights, grew a jungle of potted plants and orchids that shone like jewels.

"It is amiable of you to come and help an old man," Mr. Gonsalves said when I explained about Jon being held up at work. "My friend Jon works hard—at the center, of course, and at Luigi's Pizza, where he is one of the cooks. It is a summer job, to earn money for the university in a year or two."

Giving Bolivar another pat, Mr. Gonsalves took a big key from a chain, bowed me outside, and locked the door. Then he produced two brown paper grocery sacks. "Before we go," he said, "let us gather some flowers and vegetables for our friends at the center."

But first Mr. Gonsalves had to pull a few weeds, pick off a few Japanese beetles. Then he needed to chat with the people who came out of the other apartments to talk to him. He reassured everybody that Bolivar, who'd followed us out of a half-open window, would never hurt them. He handed out flowers and asked about his neighbors' families by name. But I noticed that though he smiled a lot, Mr. Gonsalves never laughed out loud and that he listened a lot more than he talked.

"You have some memory," I exclaimed when the

last neighbor had gone. "I'd never remember all those names."

"Names are important to people, Señorita Mai." Mr. Gonsalves put a pocket handkerchief down on the ground and creakily knelt down by the flower garden, patting earth and mulch into place around some annuals.

It seemed the friendly thing to do, so I got down on my knees beside him and started weeding, too. "Did you plant all this yourself, Mr. Gonsalves?" I asked.

"If you please, call me Hector. This garden I made when I first came to live on Arnold Street ten years ago. I was strong then. Now my kind friend Jon helps me to do the digging."

Mr. Gonsalves reached out to cup a flower gently in his brown palm. "Truly, a flower is a gift from heaven. You can see into its heart because there is no pretence in it. Ay, *scantissima*, you should have seen my garden back in El Salvador, Señorita Mai."

I said it was just Mai, no Señorita needed, and asked Mr. Gonsalves when he'd come to the States. He said eleven years ago, during the civil war in El Salvador. "We lived in a place called El Verde in the Moreza area," he told me. "Life was good, until the soldiers came to our town and shot many people they accused of being guerrillas. They killed, they tortured all day. When they left, there were few left."

"You were lucky to get away," I cried.

"Not lucky, child." Mr. Gonsalves's brown eyes suddenly held unbearable sadness. "My good wife had died some years before the massacre, but my son and my daughter—"

He broke off. "I'm sorry," I whispered, wishing I knew what to say.

"It is as God wills," Mr. Gonsalves said, but he got really quiet.

It hurt to watch him, so I kept working on the garden and finally he stirred, sighed, and suggested we pick the flowers and some tomatoes for the center.

"And you, Mai?" he asked a while later as we progressed from picking flowers to gathering veggies. "How goes your quest in Boston?"

"My what?" I asked, surprised.

"Mrs. Menzies at the Sayel Center told me that this was your first visit to Boston, that you had never met your aunt and uncle or your cousins before. Such a journey sounds like a personal quest. But perhaps it was discourteous of me to have mentioned this?"

He looked worried, so I said, no, it was okay. "I'm adopted, and I never knew I had a blood aunt and uncle and cousins before last month. I guess I'm looking for, you know, my roots."

Mr. Gonsalves nodded thoughtfully. "But remember," he added, "that roots are not the only things that bind a family." He pointed to a spiderweb that spread between his tomato plants. "That web is so delicate, yes? But strong. Tenacious. Memories and stories are like spiderwebs, and you cannot lose them, even if—"

Once again he stopped himself. I knew that he was thinking of his lost family, but even though his memories were so sad, I couldn't help envying Mr. Gonsalves. He had his "spiderwebs," and no one could take them away, whereas here I was with no memories and no stories about Mai Hongvan except for the little bit that Mr. Vuong had told me.

"It must be difficult for you," Mr. Gonsalves was saying. "To come into a family where there are no shared memories is not easy. Sometimes you are lonely, no?"

His brown eyes were so understanding that I nodded. "You must remind yourself that we are all of us interconnected with the greatest of all spiderwebs," he then said.

"How's that again?" I asked, and Mr. Gonsalves carefully placed a tomato in the bag and straightened his frail back.

"When I feel lonely," he told me, "I say to myself

like this: I say, I am Hector Cruz Gonsalves, the son of Estella and Jorge Gonsalves, born in El Salvador, now a citizen of the United States of America, a member of our world, and a small but still significant part of this great universe."

He paused to give me a shy smile. "It is, of course, not the same as having my own family, but it helps a little."

Mr. Gonsalves talked more about this idea as we walked to the center, but truth to tell, I didn't listen to everything he said. Even though his talk was interesting, the sack of veggies was heavy on my one arm, and Mr. Gonsalves himself was no lightweight, either. I kept hoping that Jon might show up along the way, but he didn't get to the center until a short time after we did.

"Can you believe Hector's garden?" he asked me. "I hear the place was a dried-out piece of dirt before he started working on it."

Didn't anyone bother or vandalize Mr. Gonsalves' pride and joy, I asked. "Maybe in the beginning, but now the neighbors all watch out for him," Jon said. "Besides, there's Bolivar, the cat from hell. He hates everybody except Hector, and he likes to play hide-and-seek in the garden. One swipe of those claws'd take a guy's hand off."

I said, maybe we needed an attack cat at the restaurant. Jon looked at me questioningly, so I explained Lien's problems.

"Everyone's stressed out," I said. "There's a lot of competition from the Jade Palace, and the Pearls make things as hard as they can because Lien won't pay protection money. So far, all they've done is dump garbage and break windows, but they've set fire to businesses that don't cooperate, so it's scary. And they're scaring customers away, too."

"What you guys need is a whole lot of new customers."

"I wish," I said.

"Sure, and why not?" Jon said, suddenly all eyes

91

and Irish brogue. "Musha and begorra, let the little people help you, colleen." Then, as I laughed, he took both my hands in his. "Close your eyes and make a wish."

Even while I was telling him now nuts he was, I was realizing that having my hands held by Jon produced a sensation a little like warm goose bumps. Weird, but nice. Definitely pleasant.

"Nuts or not," Jon said, "make a wish and believe it's going to come true." He waited a beat of time. "Did you?"

Before I could answer, Judy came back from her meeting, thus reminding me that I still had all those recipes to enter into her word processor. I got to work and stayed there until it was time to head back to Lien's private salt mines.

Nothing had changed back at the Spring Restaurant. In sullen silence Nancy waited on the few customers who either didn't care about the Pearls' ban on the place or didn't know. Then, at seven-thirty, things suddenly picked up. A party of seven—four girls, three guys—walked into the restaurant.

They were all kids about Nancy's age or a little older. "Customers," I said, but Nancy just stood there. I gave her a little shove.

"He-ey, Nancy Tranh!" one of the girls called.

"You know them?" I asked, and she got a little pink as she explained that they were kids from her high school. As she drifted over to their table, I checked the kids out. The girls were all good-looking—one was Asian, the other two looked Latino. The one who'd called to Nancy was model-pretty with curly brown hair and big hoop earrings and fluttering eyelashes that looked too long not to be fake. She wore a halter and a miniskirt that showed lots of skin.

I switched my attention to the guys—both Asian— and saw that one of them was drop-dead gorgeous, with snapping black eyes and a smile that lit up the room. He couldn't seem to keep his eyes off Nancy as she walked over to take their order. They talked and joked around for a bit, and then the gorgeous guy put an arm around Nancy's waist.

Just then Lien walked through the swinging doors into the restaurant. She took one look at Nancy and then grabbed my arm. "You go take their order," she growled at me. "You tell my daughter come here. *Now*."

"They're friends from her school," I said, but that wasn't going to get Nancy out of trouble from the look on Lien's face. I went over and told my cousin, who tossed back her long black hair and smiled down at the guy who was still holding her around the waist.

"I have to go, Ken," she said.

Her voice was soft, a caress. The guy called Ken took his arm away as if it hurt to do it. "I'll check you later, Nance," he promised.

Slowly, her hips swaying gracefully, Nancy walked away. The guy followed her with his eyes as if he could eat her with a spoon. One of the other guys said to me, "You're new here, aren't you?"

Not wanting to get into family history, I said I was the new waitress and took their order. Then I went back to the kitchen, where Nancy and Lien were snarling at each other like a couple of cats. "You stop acting like tramp," Lien was hissing in English. Her eyes were like burning coals. "Flirting with that boy. Shame on you, Nguyen!"

"Those were kids from my school. I told you," Nancy snapped back. "My *friends*, okay?"

"Not okay! You let that boy put his hand on you." Lien's clip-and-throw diction had never been so deadly. "He not even Vietnamese boy, ha? What his name?"

"Ken Sawada. He's in my English class at school."

Lien's eyes narrowed. "*Japanese*," she spat out. "You let *Japanese* boy put arm around you, ha? What kind Vietnamese girl would do such thing? You acting no better than streetwalker. No better than—"

She broke off, shot a glance at me, and then switched to high-voltage Vietnamese. "Be quiet," Uncle Diep said in an alarmed cheep, "they will hear you in the restaurant."

"I talk to you later," Lien promised. She then stalked away, leaving Nancy standing there with her fists clenched.

"Sometimes," she whispered, "I hate her! She's going to push and push me until I burst."

But I hardly heard Nancy, because I was remembering the way Lien had looked at me. When she made that crack about a prostitute, she'd been talking about Mai Hongvan.

Lien hated her dead sister. Hated her and wouldn't talk about her. She wouldn't even honor her sister's ghost on her spirit altar. I had to face facts. In Lien Van Tranh's family there were no roots and no spiderwebs that reached as far as me.

So why be a glutton for punishment? I asked myself as I worked through the long night. Why did I even bother to stay? Surely not because I wanted to be treated as an indentured servant by this bitter woman who no way wanted to be my aunt. Not to be shouted at and ordered around, either.

I'd had it. The worm had finally turned. First thing tomorrow morning, I was going to call home and tell them I was flying back to Serena.

But the next morning before the alarm clock went off, there was a knock on the bedroom door. When I stumbled to answer it, I found Vinny stand in the hall.

"Hey, Mai," he whispered, "you ready to do some serious kite-flying?"

I glanced at the alarm clock and saw it was a quarter to five. "Are you nuts?" I groaned. "It's still dark outside."

"It'll be light in a bit. Kite-flying's the greatest

when the sun comes up," Vinny assured me. "Besides, if we go now, we'll be back before Ma can get all bent out of shape."

He was all dressed and ready, and he had a rolled-up kite under his arm. "What the heck," he added, "you'll be up in an hour, anyway. Where would you rather be? At the reservoir, watching the sun come up—or here?"

Since I'd decided to call it quits as Lien's slave, Vinny definitely had a point. Hauling on jeans and an old T-shirt, I followed my cousin out of the house into the predawn grayness. "It feels great, doesn't it?" he enthused. "Cool and dark—like there's nobody alive in the world but us."

Everything was shuttered and dusky, and there was no traffic on Springvale. The shops were all closed, but as we came up to the Megabytes store, Vinny slowed his steps to peer into the window.

"That's one of the games I want to buy," he sighed.

About to say something sympathetic, I noticed that a woman had come out of the door of the Jade Palace restaurant and had commenced sweeping the steps. As she passed under a streetlight, I did a double take. The sweeper was Big Orchid.

"Hey," I called softly. "Hi, there!"

She looked up, saw me crossing the street toward her, and stopped sweeping. "Hi," I repeated, "how is your baby?" Then, remembering that this woman spoke no English, I pantomimed rocking a baby. "How is Lan?"

By now I was close enough to see the look of pure terror sweep all the color from her face. All color, that is, except for the horrible purplish bruise over one eye and cheek. For a fraction of a second we just stared at each other. Then Big Orchid picked up her broom, scuttled back into the restaurant, and shut the door.

"What's the matter?" Vinny asked behind me. "Who were you talking to?"

"Big Orchid—the woman I told you about, the one

who brought her baby to the center," I stammered. When I thought of Big Orchid's bruise, I felt sick. "Someone beat her up—"

"Well, there's nothing you can do for her if she runs away from you," Vinny pointed out. "Anyway, we'd better get going."

He started walking, but I hung back, staring at the Jade Palace and wondering who could have hurt Big Orchid. I thought of calling the police but then recalled what Dr. Sayel had said. If they were in the country illegally, my calling the police would mean even more trouble for Big Orchid and her baby.

Undecided and unhappy, I followed Vinny as he took a right onto Commonwealth Avenue. "How far do we have to walk?" I asked.

"Not far," Vinny said. "The streetcar starts running at five, so we'll take it as far as Chestnut Hill Avenue and walk to the reservoir."

Even at this early hour there were joggers doing their thing. I saw them trundling all along Commonwealth, and when we walked into the athletic field near the reservoir, a couple was working on t'ai chi. Vinny knelt down on the dew-wet grass to spread out his kite.

And it was some kite! "Did you really make that yourself?" I asked. He nodded, and I said, "You're an artist, you know that? You could be a great painter or something."

"Fat chance of that. I'm going into business, according to Ma. Or a lawyer, or a politician, or a teacher. That's why she made me go to summer school, in case you didn't figure it out—she wants me getting A's next year, like that dweeb, Phong Dinh."

While he was talking, Vinny carefully lifted up his kite and handed it to me. It was really beautiful—a red and blue scaled dragon with a pearl in its mouth. "Hold on to it," he instructed me.

He then walked away, trailing string as he went. "One time I let my kite go too fast and it tore loose and got stuck in a tree," he explained. "I don't want to lose this one—it's the best of all the kites I have. It took me months to put this guy together."

A gentle wind came out of nowhere and tugged at the kite in my hands. "Shall I let it go?" I called.

"Not yet. I'll tell you when." Vinny's smooth face was absorbed, serious. "Okay," he shouted, "now!"

I let go and held my breath as a gust of wind snatched the kite from me and chased it, flapping, into the sky. The couple doing t'ai chi stopped to watch as, above us, the dragon switched its long paper tail fiercely.

"Oh," I whispered, "wow."

Vinny took my tribute for granted. "It does look great, doesn't it?" he asked happily. "I copied it out of a book on Chinese art."

The word nudged my mind back to the Jade Palace and Big Orchid. "Vinny," I said, "could the Pearls be involved in bringing illegal workers to the Jade Palace?" Vinny shrugged. "You must know," I persisted. "You're good friends with Sammy's brother."

Vinny gave me a scornful look. "Sammy doesn't tell Tommy about gang business, Mai."

"But I thought—"

"Tommy's too young to be a Pearl. You can't belong to a gang until they let you," Vinny told me. "You've got to earn the right to be jumped in. Then you get to learn the signs and stuff that only the group knows." I asked, like what? "Oh, there's a handshake you use with brothers, you know. And gestures and, like, the CKs have this whistle they use to signal each other."

Vinny talked as if it were some kind of terrific privilege to belong to a gang. It made me uneasy, to say the least. "How do you, ah, earn this right?" I asked.

Sometimes, Vinny said, right was earned when a prospective member got in trouble with the police, or did something that gave him juice—power. "Like going to jail. Sammy's been in jail twice," he added almost proudly.

"And that makes people look up to him? That's crazy."

Vinny shrugged again, and I watched him draw his kite strings closer so that the dragon hovered over us. Now I could clearly see that the pearl in its mouth was black.

"Do *you* want to join the Pearls?" I asked bluntly.

Vinny hesitated for a moment before he said, "We weren't talking about me, remember? But I can understand why—" He broke off.

"Why what?" I demanded.

"It's life, you know?" Vinny said. "You have to defend your own space. Have to hold on to what you own. If someone picks on you, and if you're too weak to stand up by yourself, you have to get help to keep your self-respect."

In a way, I understand what Vinny meant. I'd been helpless when those skinheads spray-painted me and again when I came up against Billy Lintell. My helplessness in both cases had done zilch for my self-respect.

"Listen, it's survival," Vinny was saying. "You have to be a part of a group, or they'll run over you." Who were 'they'? I asked, the CKs? "Sure," Vinny agreed, "but the CKs aren't the only ones to watch out for. I mean, you don't have to be in a gang to see that people don't trust each other."

Vinny said that he was used to being called names at school because he was Asian. "One time some kids spat on me—spat on me right in front of the restaurant."

"White kids?"

Vinny nodded. "Yeah, they were white. But the black kids hassle us, too. One time, a bunch of them cornered me and Tommy and beat us up. They said all slopes should go back to Ho Chi Minh City."

Once again I knew what he meant. A remembered, sick feeling churned my stomach as Vinny continued. "It's all one big mess, you know? Ma doesn't trust anybody who's not Vietnamese. I mean, she's not the only one—Mr. Vuong doesn't like Cambodians and won't have anything to do with Mr. Ly. Mr. Ly doesn't like Vietnamese—probably because of Mr. Vuong. And the Filipino kids I go to school with hate the Japanese because of what the Japanese soldiers did in the Philippines during World War II—"

Suddenly, he broke off. "Ah, rats," he exclaimed.

Following his gaze skyward, I saw that the dragon kite had gotten itself tangled in the top branches of a tree growing some distance away. Its tail was flapping wildly in the wind, but a sharp branch was sticking through the dragon's mouth.

"Wind shift took it—serves me right for not paying attention to what I was doing," Vinny cried, beside himself. He pounded his fist into his thigh, muttering, "Oh, damm it, I am *so* stupid! I shoulda paid attention to that damned wind."

"Let's get it down," I said, but the tree was too tall, too skinny to climb, and the kite too firmly wedged for us to shake it loose. Even though we tried everything we could think of, we couldn't budge it.

"All the work I put into that kite—" Furious, miserable, Vinny kicked at the earth under the tree. "Ahh, what's the damn use, anyway?"

Something in the way he ducked his head and hunched his shoulders jogged a memory, and I remembered how David had looked on that hospital gurney the day he hurt himself. For some reason that memory brought tears to prickle against my eyelids.

It had been a long time since I talked to the brat or to Liz or the folks. I wondered, had they missed me? and how would Mom react to the news that I was coming home?

Chapter Seven

I PHONED SERENA after breakfast, which I ate all by myself on account of Vinny and my being in disgrace. Because of our attempts at rescuing the kite, we were late getting back to Springvale, so Lien snarled at Vinny about starting to act like a responsible almost-grown-up Vietnamese-American boy who, never mind stupid kites, should be thinking of ways to make his family proud.

Then she packed him off to do chores before summer school began. Me, she totally ignored. I could have stood a lecture. I could have dealt with being yelled at. But Lien's acting like I didn't even exist bugged the heck out of me. Fuming, I phoned Serena to tell them I was coming home *today.*

Except that nobody was home. Six o'clock in the morning, Iowa time, and nobody was home! I couldn't believe it when the answering machine came on and Dad's recorded voice began, "Thank you for phoning the Houstons. We are unavailable to take your call now, but if—"

I slammed down the receiver without leaving a message and sat around for five minutes feeling sorry for myself until Nancy came upstairs to demand what was I doing, taking a nap in the middle of the day?

"Those low-life Pearls broke another window in front and spray-painted stuff all over the street," she fumed. "The glass man's coming, and the Woman of Steel wants us to clean up the mess. That weasel, Pham, *says* he has to study for a test, and Luu isn't feeling so hot—flu or something—so you and me are elected, kiddo."

The turpentine we used to scrub out the graffiti brought bad memories. As we worked, I abruptly told Nancy that I was going back to Iowa. "So, just like that, you're quitting?" she demanded.

"Not *just like that*," I protested. "You know I've tried to fit in, but Lien doesn't want me here—never did."

"*I* want you here," Nancy came right back. "We're just getting to know each other. And Vinny took you kite-flying, which he does only with people he's closest to. How do you think he'll feel if you leave now?"

I said nothing, but my resolve was weakening as Nancy went on unhappily. "I know it's been bad here lately with Ma the way she is and our troubles with the Pearls and everything. I don't blame you for wanting to go home, but—but I wish you'd stick around, Mai. I'd have gone totally nuts without my cousin to talk to."

She sounded near tears, and I felt like crying myself. I ended up telling Nancy I'd think it over, which I did through the long morning and into the afternoon. One thought that kept coming around like abandoned luggage on the baggage-claim beltway was that if I left Boston now, I would be going home without having found out what I wanted to know about Mai Hongvan.

Which, if I were honest with myself, was what I'd hoped for yesterday when Jon told me to make a wish.

Then, that afternoon, the mailman brought me a postcard from Camp Oswego signed by everybody. Mom and Dad and David—he was hopping around on his crutches pretty well, he said—had gone up to see Liz at camp. They were going to stay at Oswego for ten days, fishing and boating and lazing around, and they hoped everything was going all right with me.

Everybody had scrawled a little message on the

101

back of the card. I tried to picture how each of them must have looked while writing to me, but noises from the restaurant kitchen, where I was reading the card, kept intruding, and instead of red-haired, blue-eyed Houstons, I thought of Vinny, and Nancy, and silent Uncle Diep, and, last but not least—

"What that you doing, Mai?" Lien's voice at my shoulder startled me so much that I actually stammered when I told her I'd got a card from my folks. "They having good time camping," Lien then said. "I bet you wish you were back home."

Dark, narrow eyes watched me from behind rimless glasses. Her mouth was as thin and as disapproving as always. "Yes," I said bluntly, "I do."

Okay, so this was it. She'd say, why don't you go home, then? and I'd say, fine, I'll go pack my bags. I was so sure that Lien would say the words that my response was already bubbling to my lips when she said, "You work hard many weeks now. You good girl. Help family a lot."

The Woman of Steel *praising* me? As I gaped at her, I saw her raise her hand, extend it so that it almost touched my shoulder, and then draw it away. "You help a lot," she repeated.

Then she turned and started chewing Pham out for cutting the chillis too thick, and criticizing Nancy, who was frying spring rolls in Luu's absence. Sure, I told myself, Lien's buttering me up because she's shorthanded with Luu out sick. She doesn't want me to leave now, or she'd really be stuck.

Even so, quiet little Serena faded gently away, and I stopped thinking of Oswego Lake as Boston traffic muscled past the Spring Restaurant's window front. An ambulance wailed somewhere in the near distance, and then the bell of the restaurant's door jangled and Jon Delaney walked in.

With him were an older man who looked exactly like him, a plump lady with strawberry-blond hair, two little boys, and a girl about Vinny's age. The blond, skinny-as-rails boys were the mirror image of each other, and the girl looked like her mother.

Nancy handed me the menus with a grin. "Jon didn't bring his family here to meet *me*," she said.

Meaning that they'd come to meet *me*. I felt butterflies dancing in my stomach as I welcomed them. "You said you could use some new customers," Jon explained, "so I rounded up a few hungry bodies."

"Starving, he means," his father said. He shook my hand gravely as he added, "I'm another Jon Delaney, Mai. Jonny talks about you all the time."

Jon looked embarrassed, and the girl rolled her eyes in sympathy. The little boys hooted and poked each other until Jon told them to knock it off, or else. "Please forgive this invasion, Mai," Mrs. Delaney said as she smiled, "but we did want to meet you."

The little boys poked each other again. Mr. Delaney pretended to scowl at them and came up with one of Jon's friendly grins instead. "Jonny says you have a younger brother, so you understand these imps," he said. "They'll do better once we feed them."

I ended up serving the Delaneys, who ordered so much food that Lien was charmed. She didn't even mind when Mrs. Delaney asked me to sit down with them and talk, which I was happy to do. I liked Jon's family—they were mellow and friendly and as easy to be with as old friends. In five minutes I'd learned that Mrs. D. was a nurse at Boston Central, that Mr. D. was an accountant for a law firm in Chestnut Hill, that Shauna was a CIT at a Y camp at a place called Houghton's Pond, that one of the twins, Timmy, wanted to be a fireman, while Scott was nuts about boats.

"It's in the blood," Mr. D. cut in. "Jonny cut his teeth on the steering wheel of the *Alba Anne*."

"That's Dad's pride and joy," Shauna explained. "He *says* it's the family boat, but most of the time him and Jonny are out in it paddling around."

"She's as sweet a twenty-footer as ever sailed." Mr. D. got a dreamy look in his eyes as he described the huge fish they'd caught just last week, and when Shauna suggested I didn't want to hear any of his fish stories, he said, "Now, now. Be respectful of the fishermen in the family, or we won't take you whale-watching this year."

"Why would anyone go and watch whales?" I wondered, and the Delaneys exchanged astonished glances.

"She's from Iowa," Jon explained. "She's never seen a whale."

"Poor, deprived child," sighed Mr. D. "This time of year, the big beauties are out at the Stellwagen Bank, feeding. They put on a show I for one wouldn't want to miss."

Jon's eyes glowed as he described fifty-ton mammals leaping out of the ocean. "It's awesome," he said. "Totally awesome." Then he added, really casually, "Want to come out with me and take a look, Mai? I don't have to be at work till six o'clock this coming Friday."

As he spoke, it registered in my thick brain that Jon had just asked me on a date. Right away I cut a look at Lien and then was annoyed with myself. Why shouldn't I have a day off? I wasn't an indentured servant. I could go whale-watching with Jon if I wanted to.

With all this in mind, I spoke up fearlessly and said I'd have to ask my aunt.

So, okay, it wasn't such a courageous move, but then, living with Lien hadn't exactly filled me with bravery. I was wondering how I was going to lay the question on her when, next morning, she gave me a perfect opening.

"We did good business Saturday night," she told all of us at the breakfast table. "Lots of new people come. Your friends, Mai, ha?"

"Nancy's, too," I pointed out. "From the Sayel Center. Dr. Sayel said that Mr. Delaney used to volunteer there, and now his son does."

"Is nice of them," Lien said. Then she added, "Mr. and Mrs. Delaney order a lot of food."

She looked positively benevolent. It was now or never. "Aunt Lien," I said, "I'd like to go whale-watching on Friday."

"Watching whale?" Lien looked bewildered. "What for you want do that?"

I explained that the Delaneys had a boat. I was about to say that Jon had asked me to go out in it, when Nancy interrupted. "Ma, Mr. Delaney and his family invited Mai to go for a boat ride and watch the whales."

Lien frowned. I said, "Actually it wasn't Mr. Delaney who—"

"Mr. Delaney knows a lot of people," Nancy edged in once again. She frowned me quiet as she added, "He really liked your food, Ma. I'll bet he'll recommend us to the law firm where he works."

As we started to clear the breakfast things, she hissed, "Are you crazy? Ma'll never let you go out on a *date* with Jon. Let her think you're going with the family."

"But that's not true," I said, troubled, and Nancy rolled her eyes at me.

"You want to be Ms. Goody-Two-Shoes and lose a chance to go sailing with your cute Irish boy?" she said. "Go ahead. Be my guest. Anyway, *you* didn't lie. I did."

Which I admit was splitting hairs, but it kept me quiet for the minute it took Lien to decide, "Okay, you can go. Friday morning not so busy anyway."

Sunday was busy, so Nancy and I didn't have much chance to talk. It wasn't until we were walking to the streetcar on Monday that Nancy said I owed her one. "If it hadn't been for me, you'd have blown your chance at being with your Irish boy," she teased.

"Quit calling him that—Jon's not *my* anything," I pointed out, and Nancy just laughed. "What about you?" I demanded. "That guy Ken Sawada was really cute. Is he your boyfriend?"

"I told you, we just go to school together," Nancy said. She shrugged her shoulders. "I'm not seeing anybody right now. I mean, how could I with the Woman of Steel on my tail all the time?"

She paused and took my hand. "So now you're staying, right?" she asked. "You're not going back to Iowa?" I said no, and she gave my hand a little squeeze. "I'm glad, really I am."

A warm feeling had started in my stomach and was spreading through me. "So am I," I said.

"Vinny will be real happy." Nancy paused to kick a flattened can out of her way. "Ma is stupid, you know? If she really wanted to keep him away from the Vuongs, she should get him the video games he wants. Then Vinny wouldn't have to go sneaking over to Tommy's all the time."

She paused a beat and then added casually, "Listen, I need you to cover for me at the center today."

"Again?" I demanded.

"I'm meeting my friends—you remember, the ones who were in the restaurant that night Ma took a fit?—at Quincy Market downtown. It's Janie Chin's birthday, and we're going to take her out, but I don't want Ma to know I was hanging out with those kids. If she asks, I was at the center, okay?"

This time Nancy was asking me straight out to lie for her. I didn't like the idea, but at the same time I understood where my cousin was coming from. My aunt the control freak was driving everybody, including me, crazy.

"So," Nancy continued, "have a nice day at the center with your boyfriend, okay?"

"There you go again," I protested. "Jon's not my boyfriend."

"Have you ever had one?" Nancy laughed as I hesitated and teased, "Sooo. This is first love."

"I am *not* in—"

"I know, I know! Right now you're only interested

in each other, but you like being with Jon. Am I wrong?"

In spite of myself, I felt my own cheeks go warm. "He's okay," I muttered.

"He's cute," Nancy corrected me. "You're lucky, you know that? Ma would have a hemorrhage if I dated anybody who wasn't a Vietnamese. Look at the way she went nuts when Ken put his arm around me! But for you it would be okay."

The warmth inside me—half pleasure, half embarrassment—fizzled. "You mean because I'm *con lai*."

"That's a sick word. Don't use it on yourself," my cousin scolded. "Anyways, who cares if you are half white and half Asian? Nobody's 'pure' these days."

I got off at Union Square and walked to the center alone. By now I was a pro at this. And when a bunch of kids—I didn't know if they were CKs or some other gang or just a bunch of yahoos hanging out—whistled and made disgusting kissing sounds, I kept walking with my head high. I ignored the insulting things they said about Asian girls and instead fantasized myself kicking them where it really hurt.

Jon was already at the center, painting a wall in Judy's office. "Where's Nancy?" he asked when I settled down to collate the cookbooks that the Family Group was producing.

As I cut and stapled, I explained that Nancy was meeting her friends at Quincy Market. "She doesn't want Lien to know," I explained.

"From what I saw of your aunt at the restaurant, she didn't look so bad," Jon said. Then he added casually, "So, did she give you the day off Friday?"

"Yes," I said, and Jon looked so pleased that I felt light-headed. Nancy would have laughed at me, but when Dr. Sayel called me into her office to say hello, I almost floated in.

The euphoric feeling didn't last long, though. It disappeared the second Dr. Sayel mentioned that the Orchids had never returned to the center.

I was disgusted with myself. I'd forgotten Big Orchid's poor, bruised face. "How could I forget a thing like that?" I groaned.

"Maybe because you're human." Looking weary, the doctor sat down and folded her long fingers together. "It's frustrating when you can't help someone."

"Isn't there *anything* we can do?"

Dr. Sayel shook her head. "If I walk into the Jade Palace and demand to see Big Orchid, she'd only be beaten again after I left. And if she *is* here illegally and I call the police, what good would I have done for her?"

"Then we have to just leave things alone?" Dr. Sayel nodded.

"It's not fair," I mumbled.

Dr. Sayel looked about to say something, then seemed to change her mind. "I understand Nancy's not here again today," she said. "Isn't she feeling well?"

"She had some stuff to do," I hedged.

The doctor said, "Mmm." Then she added, "Keep your eye on the Jade Palace restaurant, Mai. Even if there's nothing we can do right now, things might change. Meanwhile you can stay what you already are—a concerned friend."

By the end of the week Lien was having second thoughts about having given me a morning off. "Why do you have to go tomorrow, ha?" she demanded querulously on Thursday evening. "Mr. Delaney doesn't have to work on Fridays?"

Nancy fielded that one. "Maybe he's on vacation," she said. "Anyway, Ma, you promised to let Mai go."

She gave me a surreptitious wink and then a big smile. Her skin glowed like warm ivory, and her eyes were shining. Ever since that Monday when she'd taken off with her friends, my cousin Nancy seemed prettier and happier than I'd ever seen her.

"You look pretty pleased about something," I said

later, when we were sitting on the back stairs together.

"Oh, I was just thinking—" Nancy broke off, grinned suddenly. "I hope you don't get seasick tomorrow, Mai. I'll bet you've never been on a boat."

Sure I had, I told her. I'd sailed many times on Lake Oswego. "Being on a lake and on the bay are two different things," she said. "But maybe you'll luck out and it'll rain."

Friday dawned fair and warm. Jon met me and together we took the orange line to South Station, from where we headed for the Dorchester Yacht Club, where the *Alba Anne* was moored. "Isn't she beautiful?" Jon declared.

The *Alba Anne* wasn't a small boat but, compared to the other boats I saw there, it wasn't huge, either. Recalling what Nancy had said, I felt a sudden surge of doubt.

I asked if he was sure that the boat was safe. Jon looked surprised. "I keep forgetting you never saw real water before," he said. "Listen, Iowa, you're safe with me. Us Delaneys have seawater in our veins. Come aboard, and I'll introduce you to *Alba Anne*."

Jon helped me into the boat and showed me around the galley, and the small stateroom that slept four. He then sat down with me in the stern, showed me how to get into my bright orange life vest, and went over the safety precautions of the boat. Finally, he informed me that it would take about an hour of sailing due east to reach the whales' feeding grounds.

An hour? But it was too late to protest—Jon had started the motor, and we were on our way.

"You sure made a hit with the family the other night," he said as I tried to get used to the way the boat lurched whenever it hit harbor swells. "My sister likes you a lot, and the twin dweebs think it's cool you're from Iowa. Mom says to bring you home to dinner anytime. Dad's telling everybody at the firm to go to the Spring Restaurant, so hopefully business will pick up and your aunt won't be so up-tight."

I said I hoped that would happen. I was even more pleased that the Delaneys had liked me as much as I'd liked them. Still, right now, I had other priorities.

"Are there sharks out here?" I asked, nervously eyeing the dark water.

"Sure there are," he said right back. "There was this one shark back in 1799 that swallowed a bunch of important state papers whole. It was caught and cut open and the papers were there intact." I said, that was gross. "Okay, then," he said, "if you don't like shark stories, there's the story about the light-house keeper and the baby."

According to Jon, the keeper of the Hendricks Head lighthouse had come down to the shore after a terrible storm and found a box lashed between two mattresses. Inside the box was a baby boy, alive and screaming.

"What happened to him?" I asked, and Jon said he'd eventually been adopted.

I shifted on my vinyl-covered foam seat. "That's pretty cold," I said. "Just because you don't want a baby, you don't have to toss it into the sea."

"Maybe it wasn't that way," Jon pointed out. "Maybe the baby's mother didn't have a choice."

"There's always a choice."

"Do you think so?" Jon asked. "I mean, sometimes a person might make a decision that seemed right at the time and then find it to be wrong later."

"I don't know what you're talking about," I said more sharply than I'd meant to. "I'm sorry," I added. "I'm on edge, I guess."

"Because of your aunt," Jon said.

"Yes. Well, no, not really. I'm stressed because of what Mr. Gonsalves calls my quest. Did he tell you?" Jon shook his head. "You know I'm adopted, right? Well, I didn't know I had a Vietnamese family in Boston till now, and this summer a lot of stuff happened and—well, I just decided I had to know the

Tranhs better. My adoptive parents didn't think it was such a good idea—they said I wasn't thinking it through—but I came anyway, so my folks are mad at me. They haven't called me or written me except for one postcard."

"That's rough," Jon sympathized as I paused to draw breath.

"I've learned a lot about my cousins and my aunt and uncle," I went on, "but nothing about Mai Hongvan—she's my birth mother. Lien won't talk about her, and she won't show me any photographs or anything. People say I'm nothing like Mai Hongvan, so I wonder what she looked like. Who *I* look like."

I took another deep breath and looked out at the dancing pinpoints of sunlight on the water. The waves were still making little jolts under us as we crested them, but by now I'd gotten used to them.

For a long while we were both quiet, and then Jon said, "I'd wonder, too. In your shoes, I mean. I'm a dead ringer for my dad, but Mom will say stuff like 'You look like your Uncle Pat,' or my aunts will go 'You're going to be just like your Uncle Philip.' Which, by the way, is bogus, since Uncle Phil has this humongous bald spot on top of his head."

"At least," I muttered, "you know where you stand."

"Yeah, maybe. But in the end, it's *me* in this skin," Jon said.

I watched his hands on the boat's wheel. They were so sure and strong. Jon knew who he was and where he'd come from. His skin and his bones might be his own, but his family could look at him and point to relatives, living or dead. That mightn't matter to Jon, but it sure as heck would matter to me.

I chewed on this thought as we sailed eastward across the bay and didn't pay much attention to the sea stories Jon was telling me until he announced that we'd reached the Stellwagen Bank.

111

"Now what?" I asked as he slowed the boat's motor.

"Now we hang out and wait for the big guys to quit chowing down plankton and put on a show. The water might get a bit choppy now that we're cutting the motor."

Jon didn't tell the half of it. As soon as he shut down the motor, the *Alba Anne* commenced to rock and heave so badly that my stomach churned. Now I knew what Nancy had meant. Through tightly gritted teeth I asked how long before the whales showed up, and Jon said, "Anytime now."

Meanwhile, the boat rocked. It rolled. It tilted. It felt as if we were riding out the mother of all storms. And every time that darn boat moved, my insides flipped.

Once, David had coaxed me into taking him on some death-defying roller-coaster ride at an amusement park, and I'd been so sick, my stomach had seemed permanently welded to my esophagus. That was the way I felt now, only worse.

I sneaked a look at Jon and saw that he was fine, healthy, totally un-sick, and somewhat puzzled about my condition. "Feeling queasy? Try to find a fixed point on the horizon," he counseled, then broke off to shout, "Look—whale breaching off the starboard side."

A humongous black, shiny tail had erupted out of the water some distance away and was waggling at us. I closed my eyes and threw up over the side of the boat.

"Hey, you okay?" Jon stopped looking for whales and rubbed my back sympathetically. "I know it takes some getting used to, but"—his voice changed—"look—off the port bow!"

I was too busy throwing up again to remember which was starboard and which was port. If this was how Mai Hongvan had felt on her crowded boat, if she'd been as sick as this—

"She must've wanted to die," I moaned.

112

"You're not going to die." Jon sounded genuinely worried as he recommended rubbing my back. "I've got some water—or seltzer, if you'd rather—"

"*She* didn't have any water." I felt so sick that my head, my eyes, my nose, ached, and my stomach ached worst of all from vomiting. "She had to feel like I do," I moaned, "worse, maybe, because they were all weak and hungry and sick, and then the little boy had to die—"

Jon clearly thought I had lost it. "*What* are you talking about?"

"I'm talking about Mai Hongvan," I wailed. "Now I know how she felt on that boat. I didn't before. And I still don't know anything about her, and the way things are going, I never will."

I began to cry. Dimly, I felt Jon put an arm around me to comfort me. I tried to stop my tears, but instead the words came blurting out of me.

"My mom and dad and brother and sister all have red hair and blue eyes. My aunts and uncles have blue eyes, and look at me. Who *am* I, anyway?"

"You're Mai. Mai Houston."

Jon sounded puzzled, like, who else would you be? I peered up at him and felt sick again because the boat lurched, but he hung on to me, and when I fixed my eyes on him as he'd said I should do, his blue eyes met mine.

The expression I saw there told me that he really meant what he'd just said. When Jon looked at me, he didn't see an almost-Asian girl with dark hair and dark, hazel-flecked eyes or a *con lai*. What he saw was *me*.

Me, Mai Jennifer Houston.

All of this happened in a second. That fragment of time might have seemed as natural as breathing to Jon, but it was so important to me that I almost forgot to be sick.

"I never thought you'd get so sick," Jon was apologizing. "We're going to head back. I'll just—"

And then, just then, just a few hundred yards

ahead of the boat, this huge thing burst out of the water and into the sun, and here was this gigantic velvet-and-barnacled black body, a humped head, and a large, curious, rolling round eye that was looking right at me.

For a second the whale seemed suspended in space and air, and then it splashed down, bathing the *Alba Anne* and Jon and me with cold sea spray.

"Oh, wow," Jon gasped as the boat rocked in the wake of that giant body, and I held my breath, struck dumb with awe. This was one fish story that Liz and David would never, never believe.

And suddenly I wished that my brother and sister were there with me. I wished that I'd never left them, or Serena, or ever heard of a woman called Mai Hongvan, who was starting to tear my heart apart.

Chapter Eight

"SO," NANCY WANTED to know that night after the restaurant closed and we could sit on the back steps and eat oranges, "how was your date?" I said I'd spent most of the time throwing up. "I told you," she sighed. "You wouldn't get me on a boat for anything. What happened besides your feeding the fishies?"

"We talked," I said. About what? Nancy asked. "About growing up in hicksville Serena, and about Jon's family, and about Mr. Gonsalves—"

"You mean the little old gardener?" Nancy gave my arm a little pinch. "Hurry up and get to the good part. Did Jon kiss you? Did he get romantic?"

"We held hands when the *Alba Anne* got to shore," I said.

At first this was necessary—I mean, the ground under my feet felt like Jell-O—and later it just seemed natural to keep on holding hands. We'd had ice cream near the yacht club, walked inland, talking, and stopped at a kiosk, where we'd ordered hot dogs with onions, chillies, and peppers—

"Didn't you just get through telling me how sick you were?" Nancy interrupted.

"I told you I could eat anytime, didn't I? Anyway, we sat down to eat and a bee landed on my hot dog, and somehow while we were shooing the bee away, we sort of kissed. I think."

Nancy pronounced me beyond hope. Even a hick from Iowa, she said, should know for sure whether she'd been kissed or not.

I told her that the maybe-kiss really didn't matter,

anyway. "We felt, you know, close," I said, but Nancy just rolled her eyes and said she'd have to have a talk with Jon.

"Maybe the guy needs a how-to manual," she giggled, and then took off, laughing, when I threw orange peels at her.

That night I dreamed of Baby Orchid being tossed about on huge waves until a mermaid came and rescued her. The mermaid had long black hair and looked like me.

"Mai, Mai," the mermaid sang in a sweet, sad, faraway voice, "don't you know who I am?"

I woke up with a start. Nancy was fast asleep in the other bed, and the clock near my bed said four-thirty. As I lay in bed, I heard footsteps in the corridor outside. Vinny going to fly another of his kites, I figured, and was a little hurt that he hadn't asked me.

I tried to turn over and get back to sleep, but I couldn't. Finally, I got up and padded out to the kitchen to pour myself some milk and found Lien sitting there.

She was wrapped up in a pink cotton bathrobe and slippers, and there was a pink net holding in her fuzz of hair. She had a packet of papers spread in front of her on the kitchen table, and she was squinting at something through her glasses.

I was debating whether or not to sneak back to bed without her seeing me, when she looked up. "Why you up so early?" she wanted to know. I told her I couldn't sleep. "Me, neither. I made *tra*. You want to have?"

Her voice was unusually mild for Lien, so I ventured into the kitchen to pour myself a cup of hot tea from the pot on the counter. As I did so, I glanced down at the papers in front of my aunt and saw that there were photos mixed in with the papers.

Most of them were old. Some were faded, but most of the snaps were a clear black and white, and hope

116

stirred. Maybe there'd be a photograph of Mai Hongvan in that pile.

"Enjoy it," Lien said automatically as I sat down at the table with my tea. Then she sniffed. "About time I cleaned up these old things. Old bills, old letters, old stuffs. Diep is collector rat. He keep, keep, keep. Wouldn't let me throw these old junks away."

She picked up a black-and-white photo of a serious-looking man and woman in some kind of costume. "Who are they?"

"My parents," she said. "Taken on day they marry."

These strangers were my biological grandpa and grandma. It was a weird feeling. I thought of the only gram I knew, Gram Jenny, my mom's mom, with white hair, blue eyes, dimples, and a warm hug scented with Jean Naté—and then looked down at these serious young Asian faces. No matter how hard I tried, I couldn't see myself anywhere in their remote features.

Lien slid another photograph in front of me and announced, "Me and Diep when we get marry."

Even as a young bride in traditional Vietnamese bridal costume, Lien had been plain. Her face was still too long, her jaw too strong. But she was smiling, and next to her, Diep was grinning fit to beat the band.

I'd never seen my Vietnamese uncle smile, I realized, not even once. Meanwhile Lien was saying, "Here is my middle sister, mother of Gian. Her name Ha Thi."

I'd never heard of a third sister! Ha Thi had a smooth round face with Vinny's dimple and a warm smile. "Is she—ah—still alive?" I asked.

"Living in Vietnam. Ha Thi and husband didn't leave that country when we go." Lien seemed to sigh a little. "She have two children. One, Truong, is girl, marry, have three babies now. Gian Ha Thi's other child."

I felt light-headed as these thoughts sank in. I had

117

more blood cousins who lived in Vietnam. Another surprise was that from her face and the way she touched the smiling photographed face, Lien really loved Ha Thi. As she told me how cute Ha Thi had been as a baby, how she'd followed her everywhere on short, chubby legs, I wanted to ask, what about Mai Hongvan? Tell me about her, too.

But I didn't dare. I just listened as Lien told me stories about her family, let the delicate tendrils of what Mr. Gonsalves had called spiderwebs slide from Lien's memory into my own. She showed me other photos: a color print of a baby Gian Cu; a shot showing a serious boy Vinny's age—Gian again. Then there were photos of Cousin Luu as a young girl, Luu's children at their grandmother's house, and finally Pham's unmistakably scowling countenance squinting into the sun.

Lien paused to tap her forefinger on this snap. "That Pham is Diep's dead brother's only son," she told me. "He make good lawyer one day. He do good in school. Don't trust nobody."

There was grim approval in her voice and an ironic humor that made me bold enough to ask, "Don't you have any photographs of Mai Hongvan?"

Lien seemed to freeze. Then, without answering, she shoved the photos into a brown manila envelope and put a rubber band around them. Clearly, the answer was no. "But why not?" I prodded. "You have pictures of everybody else. Why don't you have any of her?"

Lien turned and looked at me out of eyes that had grown stone cold. It was as if a door that had just begun to crack open had slammed shut between us. "You better go back to bed," she directed. And then—"No use asking for photos of *her*. I tear up."

"You *tore* her photographs up?" I gasped. "Why?" There was no answer, and I plunged on. "Nancy says that you don't even have a picture of her on your spirit altar."

While I was still talking, Lien got up and carried

her packet of papers and photographs out of the kitchen. Even after her bedroom door had closed behind her I could feel in that warm kitchen the chill of her hate.

Hate for Mai Hongvan. And hate for Mai Houston, too.

I didn't know why Lien should hate us, but she most surely did. You didn't have to be a genius to figure out that she considered us outside the circle of her family. Though Lien might tie herself up into knots to help Pham and Gian Cu and eventually Luu's children, would she even lift one finger to help me?

"No way," I muttered.

A few days ago this incident might have made me throw in the towel and crawl back to Serena in defeat, but not now. Lien had hit a stubborn streak in me, and I wasn't going to budge. This bitter, mean woman had answers to all my questions, and I wasn't leaving Boston without getting them.

Which was all very fine and easy to say but hard to do, and I definitely needed advice. Monday, I thought, I'd see Jon and Mr. Gonsalves. I'd already trusted Jon with my feelings about Mai Hongvan, and I knew he'd help me sort things out. And Mr. Gonsalves would be able to guide me with his understanding of family relationships.

It worked out fine that when Nancy and I got to the center on Monday, Mrs. Menzies suggested I go and collect Mr. Gonsalves. "Jon was going to try and get there, but his work hours at the pizza parlor have changed," she explained. "If he's late, you'll have the dear man covered."

Nancy winked at me as I left the center. "Maybe you'll meet Jon on the way. It's a nice day for a nice *long* walk."

It was also a very warm day. By the time I'd trotted the two blocks to Mr. Gonsalves's house, I was perspiring. Mr. Gonsalves must have thought so, too, because his apartment door was halfway open and

119

Bolivar was prowling around on the steps that went down into the basement.

When that cat saw me he let out a blood-curdling yowl and started to stalk up the steps toward me. There was a menacing look in his green eyes and, remembering what Jon said about his claws, I was tempted to run.

Always face your troubles, never run away from them—silently thanking my mom for that unhelpful bit of advice, I tried to appear confident and called, "Bolivar, you keep away from me."

No dice—that feline kept coming straight at me, and he looked mean. "Mr. Gonsalves?" I shouted, but there was no answer. "Hey, cat, don't even think about messing with me," I then warned.

My words ended in a shriek as he rushed forward and butted my leg with his hard head. Not waiting for him to hook his claws into me, I took off and raced past him down the basement steps. "Mr. Gonsalves," I panted.

Still no answer. Perhaps he was getting dressed? I could hear an electric fan whirring someplace, and the click-click of a shade dancing in the artificial wind. "Mr. Gonsalves?" I repeated, and then added, "It's Mai."

The silence made me nervous. I walked through the kitchen, saw that a cup of coffee, half full, stood on the rickety table, and tried his name one more time.

Then I saw him. Dressed in pajamas and a ratty old robe, Mr. Gonsalves was was lying facedown on the living room floor. When I ran to kneel beside him, he looked so shriveled and gray, and his pulse was faint and scatty.

Something hard butted against my shoulder, and I found myself staring into large, unwinking green moons. Bolivar. Muttering deep in his throat, the cat stalked over to Mr. Gonsalves. He sniffed, yowled once, then came back to take a whack at my knee. *Dummy, don't sit there. Do something!*

I called the clinic on the old black phone in the kitchen and stammered out to Mrs. Menzies what had happened. Dr. Sayel came on the phone immediately, her calm voice brisk. "Don't get flustered, Mai," she commanded. "He's breathing? Good. Call 911 and I'll be there as soon as I can."

During the few minutes it took Dr. Sayel to get there, I sat by Mr. Gonsalves, held his hand, and begged him not to die. Beside me, Bolivar keened loudly and worked his claws through the threadbare rug.

Footsteps moving fast, and an urgent—"Okay, Mai—scoot." That was Dr. Sayel, and as she was examining Mr. Gonsalves, sirens wailed outside and an ambulance came screeching down the street. "I'll have him taken to Brighton Memorial, it's closest," Dr. Sayel decided.

"Will he be okay?" I asked, wanting her to tell me yes, but all she'd say was that she hoped so.

"Go back to the center, Mai, tell Mrs. M. I'm going to the hospital with Hector. She and Nate and Judy will have to manage—" A pat on my shoulder and Dr. Sayel was gone, and I stood on the front steps blinking after the retreating ambulance. As it turned the corner, Jon came pedaling his bicycle up the hill.

"What's going on?" he demanded. "Where's Hector?"

"I found him unconscious on the floor. Dr. Sayel's having him taken to Brighton Memorial." That much I managed to say quite calmly, but then I remembered what Mr. Gonsalves had been wearing and I recalled his poor bare feet, and my eyes began to fill with tears. "I wish he were dressed," I mumbled. "He'll hate looking like that at the hospital."

Bolivar howled as loud as a coyote. "It's going to be okay," Jon told me, using the words that Dr. Sayel hadn't said. "Hey, Bolivar, will you cut it out? Hector's not going to die." Then he added, "I'm going to ride down to the hospital and see what's going on. Want to ride along, Mai?"

When I told him that Dr. Sayel wanted me to go back to the center, Jon said to climb up on the back of his bike and he'd give me a ride. As we rode along he said, "Don't write the old guy off, Mai. He's a survivor."

"When I found him, I thought he was already dead." Clinging to Jon's lean middle, I pressed my face against his back, drawing comfort and strength from his warmth. "He looked so awful, Jon."

"Hey, Iowa, take it easy," he rallied me. "It could be that he didn't take his medication or something as simple as that. Doc Sayel's with him, okay? She knows what to do."

As he spoke, I heard a familiar laugh nearby and, turning my head, I saw Nancy walking hand in hand with a boy. He was Ken Sawada, the handsome Japanese boy who'd come to the restaurant one night. From the way they were talking, heads bent close, they were in a world all their own, and now they stopped in the middle of the road to kiss.

Then Nancy saw us. For a second she stood stockstill, staring at us, and then she waved. "Hey, you guys," she called.

Jon pulled up at the curb near Nancy and the boy. Really casually Nancy said, "This is Ken. Ken, meet my cousin Mai and Jon Delaney."

Jon said hi. I said hi. Nancy's boyfriend flashed me a bright smile and said, "We met at the restaurant, right?" I nodded awkwardly, and he said, "I have to thank you for covering for Nancy so we could be together."

"Come on, Kenny, we're going to be late." Nancy smiled at Jon and me sunnily. "Catch you guys later."

They walked away. "The times I covered for her, she was seeing him," I stammered. "Why couldn't she have told me she was seeing Ken?"

"That's pretty typical for Nancy." I looked at Jon

sharply. "You met her only this summer, right? When you know her better, you understand that she bends the truth a lot of times. I've heard her work Mrs. Menzies and Judy like a pro. She doesn't get much mileage out of Nate, though, and she knows better than to try it on Doc Sayel."

"What do you mean?" I didn't like the cold feeling that was forming in the pit of my stomach.

"Well, when Nancy wants time off or something, she just sort of makes up a story. She can wheel and deal—" Jon stopped suddenly and looked uncomfortable.

"Lien's the one to blame. Living with her, you have got to lie sometimes." Jon said nothing. "I mean, she is so bossy, she tells you what to do every single minute. If *my* mom was like Lien—"

I broke off. Jon started pedaling again. After a while he said, "Don't make too big a thing out of what I said, Mai. It's just the way Nancy is." But that didn't make me feel any better. My cousin, who I thought was my friend, to whom I thought I was really close, had been lying to me all this time.

Don't lie to others, don't lie to yourself—Mom had said that to Liz and the brat and me a hundred thousand times. I tried to think of her and of Dad and the kids, but they seemed shadowy and far away and could give me no kind of comfort.

Because Dr. Sayel wasn't there, things were confused at the center. Nate coped as well as he could with the waiting patients, and Judy helped him. I was up front with Mrs. Menzies, fielding phone calls while she changed appointments around, when Dr. Sayel finally walked in.

She gave it to us straight out. "It's good and it's bad. Hector's suffered a minor stroke and is partially paralyzed on his left side, but he'll be all right. The thing is that he won't be able to live alone for a while."

"If at all," Judy said from the hall. Behind her, big Nate was listening, arms folded across his chest.

123

"Exactly so." Dr. Sayel met our concentrated gaze, then straightened her shoulders and briskly walked over to her consulting room.

"What'll happen to him?" I whispered as Nate followed the doctor.

Mrs. Menzies sighed. "He'll go to Gorham Rehab in West Roxbury to start off with. Right, Judy?"

"What about Bolivar?" I asked, but nobody paid attention to me.

"After Gorham—I'll do my best," Judy was saying. "He'd hate institutional living, but what else can we do? I'll do my best to get him into one of the better places."

"But he couldn't take the cat with him, could he?" Both women looked at me. "Mr. Gonsalves would never leave Bolivar. He doesn't have any other family but Bolivar."

"Well, don't you worry about that now," Judy said. She gave me a hug. "Get on home, Mai. It's been a hard day for you."

Mrs. Menzies warmly agreed and then added, "I do hope Nancy's feeling better. She said she had a bad headache earlier and had to leave."

Late afternoon sunlight shone heavy on the road back to Lien's. My mind full of Mr. Gonsalves's problems, I mechanically put my token into the streetcar and got off at Harvard Avenue. I was trudging back to the Spring Restaurant when I heard my name being called.

Nancy was standing ahead of me in the road, waiting for me. "You're late," she said. "Was it a rough day at the center?"

Right then I almost hated my cousin. "You could say that," I snapped. "Mr. Gonsalves is at Brighton Memorial, and Dr. Sayel was with him most of the afternoon."

"Ouch," Nancy said. Then she added, "Why are you so mad at me?"

She spoke so easily, smiled so coaxingly, her pretty head turned toward me as if we were sharing a terrific secret. I took a deep breath and said, "You lied to me, Nancy."

Prepared for her to be defensive or apologetic, even angry, I was surprised when she just shrugged. "I figured it was better that you didn't know the whole truth," she said. "I know you're not used to hiding stuff, and I was afraid that Ma would take one look at you and find out about Ken."

"I thought we were friends," I cried.

"Sure we are," Nancy said quickly. "I'd never lie to you if it was *important*. I was going to tell you about Ken, too. Honestly, I was. I mean, you're the only person I'd *want* to tell my secrets to."

There was an earnest look in her pretty, dark eyes, and I remembered what Jon had said about Nancy "working" people. Then I pushed the thought away. Jon had to be wrong, because right now Nancy was being totally sincere.

My cousin went on. "I'd really feel awful if you didn't believe me. You don't think I'm a bad person, do you, Mai?"

She caught my hands in hers and smiled up at me hopefully. "I swear, I'll never ever tell you even a half-lie again," she went. "Come on, say you forgive me, say we'll still friends."

It was no use. I couldn't stay mad at Nancy. "Okay," I muttered.

Nancy gave me a quick hug. "I really want you to meet Ken," she bubbled. "He was brought up in America, but his father's a Japanese businessman. A *rich* businessman, and—oh, my gosh, look at the time. We'd better hurry, or Ma will hit the roof. We'll talk later, okay, and I'll tell you everything."

"Gian Cu is all set to leave Ho Chi Minh City for Hong Kong. From Hong Kong, he will arrange to fly to America."

Lien made the announcement at breakfast a few days later and paused proudly for our reaction.

Nobody cheered. Pham buried his nose farther

into the thick book he'd brought to the table, and Diep remained wrapped in his newspaper. Vinny didn't look up from his Cheerios.

"When's he coming?" Nancy asked.

Lien beamed at her. "He will tell us when he get to Hong Kong," she said. "Soon, Ha Thi's son will be here. Probably he will come while Mai is still in Boston."

I couldn't believe it. Lien had actually used my name. She'd really smiled at me. For a second she had even looked at me as if she liked me, as if I weren't the *con lai* that she'd tried to forget about all these years.

"You work real hard," Lien was saying. "I tell Gian Cu so. He better appreciate what his family do for him, ha?"

She nodded to me, and for the first time since coming to Boston I felt included. A slow, warm curl of happiness spread through me, but it didn't have time to grow as Vinny said, "If we've made all that money for Gian, can we have a day off from working at the restaurant?"

The smile disappeared like magic. The Woman of Steel was back on track. "You crazy? No time to stop work," Lien decreed. "We got to make house ready. Got plenty to do."

Readying the house took the better part of the week. Aunt Lien must have figured this was as good a time as ever to start her yearly cleaning, because everything in the house and the restaurant was scrubbed, vacuumed, dusted, or washed. When we got a long distance call from Hong Kong saying that Gian was going to arrive at Logan on Sunday—less than a week away—things really heated up.

Right away Lien gave commands that the second bed in Vinny's room be vacated. Pham complained, whined, argued, and finally started hauling his stuff out of the room he and Vinny had been sharing so that he could move in with another Vietnamese family.

126

"All this time I'm working for this guy's passage," he was mumbling when I met him on the stairs one afternoon, "and now he shows up and it's, 'Move out your stuff, pack your bags.' I'm sent out of the house like a stray dog."

"You had your turn. Lien brought *you* over, too," I reminded him, and he gave me a hating look.

"Look who's talking," he sneered. "They moved poor Luu out for you, Your *Highness*. She had to go live with the Dings, whom she doesn't really know and who make her feel like a charity case. You're in Lien's good books right now, but it won't last. Wait till she throws your ass onto the street."

He went off, grumbling to himself, and left me wanting to kick him and at the same time understanding how he felt. I knew from experience what it was like to be on the outs with Lien.

At the moment she was in an unusually good mood where I was concerned, so I asked her if I could take off and see Mr. Gonsalves. "The stroke left him paralyzed on his left side," I explained. "Some of us from the center are going to try to cheer him up."

It was good to leave the cleaning and the complaining for a while and carry a pot of bright African daisies down to Brighton Memorial, where Jon met me in the lobby, hefting *his* potted plant as if it were a football.

"Judy already went up—she's running late for a meeting," he said. Then he added, "What's wrong with you? You look kind of green."

Hospital smells and sounds made me remember David's accident. I told Jon, who asked, "So how is your brother feeling now?"

I said, as far as I knew, David was getting along fine. Maybe he was even out of his cast by now. "You mean you still haven't heard from them?" Jon wondered.

When I thought about it, it seemed weird even to me. I'd spent nearly the whole month of July and part of August in Boston, and I'd spoken to Serena only once on the phone. And I'd had only that one postcard from them.

"Mom said she wouldn't interfere with what was happening out here." Defensively I added, "I wanted it this way, remember? I asked her to leave me on my own while I was here."

"No fooling?" Jon sounded envious. "There's no such word as privacy in my family's vocabulary. I mean, if you're in your room for half an hour, one of them's banging at the door. And, man, if I was out of state, they'd be calling every day and sending brownies by the truckload. You're lucky, Iowa."

Maybe the Houstons got tired of you, a sneering voice whispered in my mind. *Maybe they figure it's a good thing that you're with your Vietnamese family.*

To shut up the disquieting voice, I asked about Mr. Gonsalves. "He's regained some of the use of his left arm and he's going to Gorham Rehab on Friday," Jon told me as we rode the elevator up to the fifth floor. He added that Judy had put Mr. Gonsalves's name down at several places that handled long-term care but that they had long waiting lists.

"So where can he go?" I asked. Unhappily, Jon related Mr. Gonsalves would probably have to go to whatever nursing or convalescent home was available.

"But don't talk about it in front of him," he warned. "He knows about it but doesn't want us to know he knows—if you get what I mean."

In gloomy silence we followed a corridor around till it came to Room 526, where we found Mr. Gonsalves propped up in a bed talking to Judy. He looked smaller and very pale, as if coming to the hospital had bleached and shriveled him.

But when he saw us, he tried to smile in his old way. *"Hola,* my friends," he called. "It is good to see you. Tell me, how is my Bolivar?"

Though he admired the flowers we brought, he was most concerned about his cat and kept circling the conversation back to Bolivar. "Jon, it is good that you are feeding my old caballero for me," he said, then added anxiously, "but how is he? Is he sad, do you think? Does he eat well?"

Assured that Bolivar looked as mean as ever and ate like a horse, Mr. Gonsalves shook his head. "I'm worried about him. He must wonder where I am and why I do not return. Señora Judy has been saying that once he even walked down to the center to look for me."

He slapped his left leg, adding impatiently, "Ah, *scantissima*, I am like an ancient fish, drying slowly on the beach."

Judy had to leave to meet a client, but Jon and I stayed with Mr. Gonsalves for an hour. He did his best to forget about Bolivar and asked me about my "quest," and I told him about Gian Cu finally coming to America. "So you rediscover the connections in your family," he murmured. "You are fortunate indeed—"

When we finally had to go, he held onto our hands for a long time. "Watch out for him, my old *gato*," he said, and when I saw the tears in his eyes, I had to leave the room really quick because I felt like crying myself.

Jon chewed his lip as we rode the elevator down. "I can't stand it," he exploded. "A great old guy like that, and he's got the lousiest luck. First he loses his family in a filthy civil war, and now he loses the use of his left arm and leg. And now he's going to lose his cat, too, because no nursing home is going to take an animal in. If that's not the pits, tell me what is."

I asked, could Bolivar be adopted, but Jon said, no way. "That's a one-man feline if I ever saw one," he said gloomily. "He barely tolerates me, even. Without Hector, Bolivar'll probably go back to being an alley cat again, and it'll break Hector's heart."

Jon said he'd stop by every day before or after work and see Mr. Gonsalves. But though I resolved to see our friend often myself, I couldn't manage another hospital visit. As Gian Cu's arrival neared, Lien went absolutely hyper. She worked us night and day with the result that Nancy and I didn't even make it to the center that week.

By the time Sunday arrived, we were all too exhausted to react when Lien directed us to keep the restaurant going so that she and Uncle Diep could meet Gian at the airport.

"It wouldn't kill you to close the place for one afternoon," Nancy pointed out. Lien looked at her as if she'd lost her mind. "Okay, okay. So we'll man the fort."

Lien frowned, not understanding, so I translated, "We can manage."

My aunt didn't bother to acknowledge my words. She hardly seemed to notice any of us were alive. She was such a bundle of nerves, fiddling with the buttons on her navy blue dress and fussing with her purse, that just looking at her made my own stomach feel queasy. She even had put on a hat for the occasion, a flat, ugly, white hat with a dark blue rose on it. It lay on top of her head like a pancake and mashed her frizzed hair flat.

"Ma looks like she's going to a wedding," Nancy observed.

"Or a funeral," Pham sneered. Cousin Luu showed the gold tooth and muttered, *"Tok, tok,"* under her breath.

When Lien and Diep had driven off in the pickup, we all got to work. Lately the list of regulars had begun to increase, and the Sunday brunch crowd was really respectable. I helped take orders and serve, meanwhile trying to control my stomach. Far from settling down after Lien's departure, my internals were starting to feel as they had on the day of the whales.

While I was working, Vinny's stringbean friend, Tommy Vuong, came hefting a big cardboard box through the swinging doors into the kitchen and asked where Vinny was. "I need to talk to him for a minute," he said.

Tommy must have known that Lien was out, or he'd never have ventured into the Spring Restaurant. Pham snarled, "Can't it *wait*? We're kind of busy right now, junior, in case you can't see."

Because I liked Tommy and loathed Pham, I found Vinny loading the dishwasher and called him over to see his pal. I then took over loading the dishwasher until Nancy saw me and said, "That's Vinny's job. Where is he?"

"Maybe he's playing with the traffic on Commonwealth Avenue," Pham gibed. Nancy glared at him.

"I have had it with that Pham," she gritted out. "He thinks he's the boss when Ma and Papa aren't here." She raised her voice. "Chop those vegetables smaller, okay, Pham? We're not feeding beavers here."

Pham curled his lip but didn't bother to reply. "Where *is* that kid?" Nancy went on irritably. "I need him to wait tables."

I told her that Tommy had come by and that they'd probably gone outside a second to talk. "Well, the second's up," Nancy declared. "Go tell my baby brother to haul his butt back in here."

Vinny wasn't out on the back stairs, so I gathered he and Tommy were up in his room. I called up the stairs, but there was no answer. Mentally cussing Vinny out for giving me trouble, I climbed the stairs.

"Vinny," I yelled, "you better get down here."

There was no answer except for a muttering that came from Vinny's room. "It's okay, man," I then heard Vinny say. "It's okay. I'll do it for you."

The door to his room was half open, so I looked inside. Vinny and his friend were sitting on his bed with Tommy's cardboard box between them. "What are you guys doing?" I demanded.

Vinny started to open his mouth, but Tommy was quicker. He gave me his friendly grin and said, "I just brought my new video stuff to show Vinny. It's really cool."

I said, it wasn't going to be cool if Nancy caught them, and that if he was smart, Vinny'd make tracks to the kitchen. "I'm going," he said, jumping up. "Later, Tommy."

"Okay, man. Thanks, huh?"

Tommy Vuong held out his hand. Vinny took it, and they did this strange, twisting handclasp thing. "Aren't you taking your box with you?" I asked Tommy.

"I can't. My old man made me promise, no more video games, or else." Tommy pulled a comical face. "I don't want him or Ma mad at me, so Vinny says he'll keep the stuff for me. Eventually I can talk the old guy into seeing things my way."

Knowing Mr. Vuong, I figured Tommy was right. I turned to follow Vinny, who was clattering his way downstairs, and my head—and the room—took a sudden spin. "Whoops," Tommy went, catching me from behind as I staggered. "You been drinking something besides tea, Mai?"

Very funny. I went downstairs and through the kitchen door and found Nancy and Pham screaming at each other. "I don't care who you think you are, you jerk," Nancy was shouting. "My folks left me in charge, and you'll do as I say or like it."

To which Pham shot back, "Yes, ma'am, sure, head-honcho *dai lo*. You know what you can do? You can kiss my royal ass."

Dai lo. Gang leader. Suddenly, I felt dizzy again because I'd only then remembered where I'd seen that funny, flippy kind of handshake that Vinny and his friend had just exchanged. The Pearls outside my window had used it on the night Vinny came in through the window in our room.

The gangs have signs that only members use—I remembered the frustration in Vinny's voice and the longing, his hopelessness when his kite got trapped in the tree, and the way he'd said, "Sometimes, that's the only way to get ahead, you know?"

Slow I might be, but now even I had the picture. My little cousin was involved big-time with the Pearls!

Chapter Nine

I RUSHED OVER TO Nancy, grabbed her arm, and literally dragged her out of the kitchen into the back hall.

"Vinny's mixed up with the Pearls," I stammered.

She stared at me as if I'd grown another head. "What are you, crazy?" she gasped.

I told her about the carton Tommy'd brought over and about the handshake I'd seen them exchange.

"That's nothing," Nancy scoffed. "Tommy saw his big brother use that handshake and taught it to Vinny. They're just being copycats. Besides, Tommy's just a kid. Kids don't join gangs."

"Not even if he's a gang member's brother? Not even if he gets 'juice' somehow—maybe by helping the Pearls steal stuff?" Nancy frowned as I reminded her, "Tommy works part-time at Megabytes. It'd be really easy for him, wouldn't it, to help his brother and his friends break into the store?"

"First Pham acts like loony tunes, and now you." Impatiently, Nancy jerked her arm out of my grasp. "Even if Tommy did something stupid, that's got nothing to do with Vinny, okay? So stop being crazy and let's get back to work."

"Vinny's arm was all cut up one night," I persisted. Nancy, her hand on the doorknob, turned and frowned at me. "He said he'd scratched himself on a nail at the Vuongs', but I'll bet anything he was hanging with the Pearls. Maybe they tangled with the CKs . . ."

Nancy's eyes narrowed. "Vinny wouldn't be that

stupid. But you could be right—Tommy's in trouble and Vinny's covering for him."

Suddenly, she hit her thighs with her clenched fists. "Oh, damn that stupid, crazy kid. Why would he get mixed up with the Pearls after everything they've done to us?"

"Maybe that was the reason," I said. "He may think that if he's part of the group, the Pearls will leave the restaurant alone. Besides, Vinny's wanted video games for a long time, only he couldn't afford them."

Just then Pham stuck his head out and said in his most sarcastic way, "Would *Madam* come back and tell us lowly life-forms what to do?"

"I'm coming." When Pham's head disappeared, Nancy lowered her voice. "Don't do or say anything to anyone, okay? Not even to Vinny. I want to talk to him first."

As I trailed her unhappily back into the kitchen. I recalled everything I'd learned—mostly from listening to Nate talk at the center—about gangs since coming to Boston. I knew that they weren't just about turf or status but also about power and drugs and violence, and once you joined them, like the song says, you could never ever leave.

Except by death.

"When you quit daydreaming"—Pham's voice broke into my thoughts—"here's a plate of *bo nuong kim tien* some jerk at table four ordered."

My stomach twisted at the smell of the cooking, but I carried the plate of beef rolls through the swinging doors and was in time to see Nancy talking to Vinny. I couldn't hear what she said, but Nancy looked mad and so did Vinny. He stopped clearing his table and stomped off past me, not even turning around when I called his name.

I wanted to ask Nancy what she'd said to him, but we were really busy all afternoon, and before we knew it, the brunch crowd was gone and the dinner rush began. I was wondering what was taking Lien

134

so long to get back from the airport, when two guys in suits walked into the restaurant. They looked around, and the taller of the two said, "Who's in charge here?"

He flashed a badge as he spoke—Boston PD. My heart did a cartwheel, but Nancy calmly introduced herself and said, "My parents aren't here right now, so I guess I'm in charge. How can I help you, officers?"

She was smiling her pretty smile, looking sweet and anxious to please, but neither of the men looked impressed. The shorter one, a pudgy, doughboy type, announced rudely, "We're looking for Vinh Tranh. He here?"

"Vinny?" Nancy's eyes widened as if in surprise. "No, my brother's not here. Is something wrong, officer?"

"We'd like a word with him, miss," the taller cop said. "I'm Detective Gimball, and this is Detective Larkin."

Last time I'd looked, Vinny was in the kitchen. Knowing that as well as I did, Nancy told the detectives that Vinny had left the restaurant to do some errands. "He drove out to Wellesley a while ago. Is there something I can do to help you, detectives?"

"Your brother's suspected of being involved in a robbery last night at the Megabytes electronics store." Larkin, the doughboy, turned cold, pale eyes first on Nancy and then at me. "If either of you knows where he is, you'd better tell us."

"Do you know where Vinny is?" Nancy asked me. I shook my head. "If you could come back when my parents are home, it might be better," she added to the detectives.

Ignoring her, the doughboy walked through the swinging doors into the kitchen, and we could all hear him demanding to know where Vinny was. All around us diners were craning their necks to see what was going on, and those closest to us listened in as Detective Gimball asked questions: Where had

135

Vinny been last night? Were we sure he'd been at home in bed? Was Vinny friendly with Tommy Vuong?

Just then, the doughboy reappeared at the swinging doors. "Sam, come in here," he directed, "and bring those girls."

There was by now a mutter of uneasy excitement running through the Spring Restaurant. Nancy gave everyone a reassuring smile as we went to the kitchen, and then caught hold of my arm.

"Don't tell them *anything*," she whispered in my ear. "As far as you know, Vinny and Tommy know each other only from school. Period. They're *not* close."

"They'll know that's not true. All they have to do is ask around," I whispered back, and she pinched me so hard it hurt.

"Follow my lead and do like I do, understand? We've got to protect Vinny."

Her eyes were stony—Lien's eyes. My stomach lurched so hard, I thought I'd throw up then and there, and the smells in the kitchen didn't make me feel any better. Here Pham, arms folded across his skinny chest and his face a surly mask, was standing with his back to the stove. Luu, her hands shaking, was frying spring rolls.

"This one doesn't know where Vinh went, either," the doughboy said, indicating Pham with his thumb. "The woman can't speak English. What about *you*?"

I tried not to flinch as he snapped suddenly around to face me. "You Vinh Tranh's sister, too?" he demanded, and when Nancy said no, I was his cousin, Mai, the doughboy said, "You know where he is, don't you?"

I shook my head. Nancy protested, "Look, none of us knows where my brother is, but he's done nothing wrong. None of us has. We're a close family, we work really hard—"

"Sure, sure," Larkin snapped. "You're all angels, and I own the Brooklyn Bridge."

He cut back to me again. "Does your cousin belong to the Pearl gang?" he barked. Again I shook my head. "Cat got your tongue?" Larkin snarled then. He shoved his face inches from mine. "You just off the boat, or what? Maybe if we take you downtown, you might start remembering how to talk."

Apparently remembering that he was going to be a lawyer someday, Pham protested that this was harassment. Gimball told his partner to back off. Then he asked me if I knew anything that could help their investigation.

"N-no, sir," I whispered.

Gimball lowered his voice in a confidential, almost friendly tone. "See, we've been watching the Pearls for a while now, and we know that they're a fairly new, local gang. We always watch Asian gangs, Mai, because they have a potential for violence. Among other things, Pearls have been arrested for breaking into people's homes—their own people's homes, mind you—and for demanding money at the end of a gun. They also extort money from area businesses."

He smiled at me in a kindly way. "I just want you to understand who we're dealing with here. Recently, the Pearls have been involved in a series of robberies on area businesses, but they've covered their tracks too carefully. We know they're responsible but couldn't prove it till now."

"Oh, for crying out loud, spit it out," Larkin the doughboy snapped. "We're looking for some stolen equipment—a VCR, CD players, a bunch of video games—that were stolen from that electronics store on the corner, Megabytes, early this morning. Vinh Tranh or his friend Tommy Vuong brought some of the stolen goods here."

"Now, Bruce, we don't know that for sure," Gimball protested. He turned back to me, adding earnestly, "If Vinh is innocent, Mai, I'm sure you'd like to see his name cleared."

I knew what the detectives were doing. I'd seen enough cop shows on TV to realize that their "good

137

cop bad cop" routine was old stuff. But right now it didn't feel like old stuff—it was scaring me to death.

"Your cousin may be in serious trouble," Good-cop Gimball went on seriously. "We don't think he's deeply involved yet—he's on the edge of the action—so there's a chance for him to get out before he sinks with the rest of them. Know what I mean?"

He bent closer to me, but Nancy stepped between us. "Leave us alone," she snapped. "I told you my brother's not involved, and he's not here, either, so please go away."

Totally ignoring Nancy, Gimball kept his eyes trained on me. "*Have* you seen anything like that around, Mai?"

"I *told* you—" Nancy began, but Gimball said he was asking me, not her. There was an edge to his voice and now his eyes seemed to be boring into my mind, exposing all that I knew or suspected. My head ached, my stomach churned, and the room lurched and spun.

"N-no," I whispered. "No, sir."

"What's that you said?" Larkin rapped out. "I couldn't hear you, girl." I repeated what I'd said. "Know what'll happen to you if you suppress evidence? You're lying, and you know it."

I *wanted* to lie to protect Vinny, opened my mouth to do it, but couldn't get a word out my constricted throat. All I could do was shake my head.

Eyes narrowed, Larkin barked, "Tommy Vuong and your cousin are in this together. Where did they hide the stuff they stole from Megabytes?"

Lie, Nancy's eyes commanded. I willed myself to do just that, to say that I hadn't seen anything suspicious. I opened my mouth, but nothing came out except a croak.

I wished myself dead when Gimball nodded as if satisfied. "We'd like to search the house," he said, and now he wasn't looking sympathetic at all.

Nancy's head snapped back, and her mouth grew as tight as Lien's ever had been. She shook her head no, and Pham snapped, "Not without a warrant, you won't."

When the detectives had gone, promising to be back, Nancy turned on me like a rattlesnake. "How could you?" she spat out. "How could you betray your own cousin?"

"I didn't tell them anything."

"All you had to do was say you hadn't seen any electronic stuff. I *told* you what to say, but there wasn't a word out of you," Nancy raged, "and that jerk Larkin knew I was lying."

"Don't you know that Little Miss Goody-Two-Shoes cannot tell a lie?" Pham sneered. "The *con lai* thinks she's better than anyone else."

"You stay out of this—" I started to say, but Nancy stopped me.

"Pham's right. You're a snitch—a sneak! You think you're so damned moral, you couldn't lie to protect Vinny, huh? And your ma a bar girl, a slut who slept with every American GI she met—"

I slapped her hard. "You bitch," Nancy yelped, and then she jumped me.

I went over backward, hitting the counter with my head. *"Coi chung!"* Luu shrieked, imploring us to watch out as hot oil sloshed over the edges of the pan. Paying her no mind, we hit and scratched at each other and pulled fistfuls of hair. Nancy was smaller than me, but she was tough and wiry, and her long nails raked me as she cursed me.

"Stop!"

Rough hands pulled me away from Nancy, and Uncle Diep's incredulous face stared down. "What this you do?" he gasped.

Pham was holding Nancy back. Behind him I saw my aunt and the petrified face of a newcomer with a Beatles-type haircut—Cousin Gian Cu. He looked ready to bolt back to Vietnam.

"Nguyen," my aunt was gasping, "you crazy in head?"

She lapsed into a stream of Vietnamese. Nancy

answered in English. "Mai's fault—she started it," she panted. "What was I supposed to do, Ma? She told lies about Vinny and got him in trouble with the police."

Lien's face, under its pancake hat, had gone red. Now it bleached to gray as she tried to understand what was going on. "You tell me what happen," she demanded. Both Nancy and I spoke at once, and she pointed at Nancy. "First you."

Nancy launched into accusations. "Mai stole video games from the Megabytes store and hid a box of stuff under Vinny's bed," she shrilled. "The police know about it, and now they think Vinny's a thief."

"You're lying!" I wanted to shout, but my words came out in a dried-out little gasp. "Tommy Vuong brought a box of video games to Vinny so he could keep it. I never stole anything. What would I want with that kind of stuff?"

"You were going to give the video games to your boyfriend," Nancy accused me. "Ma, she's been dating an Irish boy she met at the center. You know, Jon Delaney—the one who brought his folks to the restaurant that time. I didn't want to tell you because I didn't want to get Mai in trouble."

"That's true," Pham agreed. "Mai's a big liar, Lien."

"Go upstairs, look under bed," Lien directed Diep. As he hurried out of the kitchen, I tried to give my version of the story. Nobody listened. Nancy was telling Lien again how I'd betrayed Vinny. Pham was nodding his head to every lie Nancy told. Luu was shaking her head gloomily, eyeing me and muttering, "*Xau, xau*—bad, bad," under her breath.

"You're the ones who are lying," I shouted into the noise. Lien's hard eyes bored into mine, but before I could get out more than two words, Uncle Diep burst into the kitchen with the box Tommy had brought. He put it on the middle island, tore it open, and pulled out a bunch of video games and other electronics stuff.

"So," Lien said, grimly, "it's true."

"It *isn't!*"

But she didn't even hear me. "You see this Ireland boy behind my back?" she demanded.

"Yes, she did," Nancy shouted before I could get a word in edgewise. "You can call the center. Mrs. Menzies will tell you how they took off together all the time. Mai asked me to cover for her all the time, asked me to lie to Dr. Sayel, too."

It was Nancy who had asked me to cover for *her*! Once more I tried to speak in my own defense, but Lien refused to listen. "Enough," she declared. "You bring disgrace to my family. It is mistake you come. You will go back Iowa tomorrow."

Uncle Diep turned his head away. I glanced at Pham, who was watching me with malicious pleasure, at Luu, who avoided my eyes, and then at Nancy's vindictive face. "What I can't forgive," my cousin said, "is that you pretended to like all of us."

"Get out of here," Pham jeered.

Dumb, blind, and stiff-legged with hurt, I stumbled out of the kitchen door into the hall, and then through the green door outside onto the steps. It was just turning to dusk, and a sickle moon hung low in the sky, pale behind the haze of pollution that rose from the steaming hot city.

But it wasn't bad air that made it hard to breathe. My chest felt as if it'd been crushed, and I was sick and dizzy. I heard a harsh explosive sound and knew it was me, sobbing.

Stupid, I called myself. *Dummy. Jerk.*

I'd been *so* stupid to come to Boston. How could I ever have hoped to find a part of me with the Tranhs? The past, as Lien had said long ago, was finished, and in their present lives this family had no room for me. Lien had never accepted me, and now even Nancy hated me because I hadn't done what she'd wanted me to do.

There was the sound of the green door opening behind me. I didn't want to face any of *them* again, so

141

I ran down the stairs and onto Springvale Street. Not toward busy Harvard Avenue, where a lot of people would be out walking on this fine summer evening, but down Springvale and then right onto Park Vale Avenue.

Did I have any idea where I was running to? No, but I had a vague idea that if I didn't slow down, I wouldn't have to think about what just happened.

But like dogs snapping at my heels, my thoughts followed me anyway, raced with me around the twists and turns of Park Vale Avenue. Like the poor Orchids, I'd been tolerated only because I could work. I'd been just a pair of hands to help Lien accomplish her goal of getting Gian Cu to America. Beyond that I was nothing, meant nothing. No, worse than nothing. The Tranhs hated me—maybe because I brought memories of Mai Hongvan, who'd disgraced them by producing a *con lai*, or maybe because they despised me for myself.

The Tranhs and I shared dark hair and eyes, but that was all. They'd made it clear I didn't belong with them. Maybe Billy Lintell was right, and I didn't belong anywhere.

"Where you headin', sweet-cheeks?"

The lip-smackings and whistles that accompanied the mocking question pierced the haze of my misery, and I realized that my crazed running had brought me almost the twisting length of Park Vale. There, just ahead of me, was Ringe Street, which connected Park Vale and Heather avenues.

Never go near Heather or Ringe—it's CK territory. As Vinny's long-ago warning filled my mind, I saw that a group of guys were standing against a shadowed doorway, watching me. I didn't need to see the bloodied sword on their T-shirts to know who they were.

I was alone, in the dark, and smack in the heart of CK turf. Misery over what had just happened faded before the reality of what could happen now. I had to get *out* of there, fast.

142

Vinny, that master of defensive moves, had taught me that if in doubt, I should always run back the way I came. Heart scraping against my ribs, I whirled around and started back down Park Vale.

"Why are you runnin' away from us, baby?" a voice taunted.

Looking over my shoulder, I saw that the guys had eased themselves away from the steps and were following me. They weren't hurrying or anything—they knew they could catch up to me anytime. Right now they were just having fun.

Knowing I shouldn't run, I did so, anyway. With those evil CK whistles behind me, with kissing noises to put breath in my burning lungs and push my aching legs forward, I ran. Now I was praying to meet someone, anyone, because someone *had* to be coming up this street—someone had to be on their front porches or walking out of their houses.

But there was no one. Savage laughter swirled up the deserted street, making me desperate enough to run up a flight of stairs and pound on a door. Nothing happened. I slammed my palm onto the doorbell, heard its buzzing mingle with the TV noises I heard inside the house.

No one came to the door. "Help me," I shouted, and rattled the doorknob, but it was locked tight.

"We'll take care of *you*, baby!"

I ran down the steps and out onto the street again. Now I could hear my own sobs mixing with the things the CKs were telling me they'd do to one of the Pearls' girlfriends once they caught me. There was no hope of outrunning them unless—

A car.

A car was coming up Park Vale Avenue, driving really slow. I jumped into the middle of the street, waving my arms like a mad person, and pleaded, *begged* for it to stop, but it swerved around me and peeled away. I caught a glimpse of a man and a woman in the front seat, their faces closed and frightened. "Stop—please! Help me!" I shouted after them.

More laughter spewed behind me, and I ran again until I saw a second car coming toward me around a twist in the street. Even knowing that this one wouldn't stop, either, I still did my desperate dance in front of it. It started to swerve around me as the first car had done, but then it braked so hard that the car body jounced on its wheels.

"Coi chung," I heard someone shout.

Vietnamese! As the thought sank in, I realized that this car was full of Asian guys and that the one in the front seat next to the driver was Sammy Vuong.

Almost before the thought formed, Sammy stuck his arm through the open window and started to shoot. Behind me, there was a yell from the CKs: "Pearls!"

There was a pile of garbage sitting on the curb near me, and I dived for it, scrunching my big self tight behind the sacks of trash as the car doors flew open and other Pearls tumbled out. Two guys were unfamiliar, but the third was tall, skinny Tommy Vuong. And the fourth—

"Vinny!" I shrieked.

"Get the gook bastards!"

Shots and the *ack-ack-ack* of a semiautomatic weapon savaged the air. Tommy Vuong yelled in pain, and fell facedown onto the sidewalk. Next, Vinny dropped beside him.

Screaming my cousin's name, I jumped up from behind my sheltering garbage can and darted over to where Vinny was lying. Gunfire sprayed the side of the buildings around me, and I screamed again, my voice disappearing into the craziness. The Pearls were shouting, spraying fiery bullets as they ran forward. The CKs were shooting back. And Vinny—

Vinny wasn't dead. He was crouching beside Tommy, trying to drag him to safety. I screamed at Vinny, telling him to get *down*, and when he didn't,

144

I threw myself on top of him, pushing him flat on the ground next to Tommy.

Bullets spat inches over our heads. Vinny was shouting something about Tommy needing a doctor, but I wouldn't let him wriggle free. I just wrapped my arms around him, covering him as best as I could.

"Stay *put*—" As I shouted the words, I felt something tug at my left arm. A second later there was a searing pain that began between my wrist and elbow and radiated through my entire arm.

Meanwhile, Vinny was shouting in my ear. "They shot Tommy. Mai, the CKs shot Tommy. I'm s-so scared—"

Scared? I was beyond scared. I was sure we'd be shot, too. I was sure that there was no way we could get out of there alive until I heard the sirens wailing down from Union Square. "We're *out* of here," I heard someone shout.

Shots ceased as the sirens drew closer, and from where we crouched, we could hear running feet and Sammy Vuong protesting loudly that he wasn't going anywhere without his brother. Then there was a volley of rapid Vietnamese, and the car door slammed, and it took off down Park Vale, burning rubber.

"Is it over?" Vinny whimpered.

He was as white as paper and shaking, and his eyes were huge under his fringe of dark hair. There was blood on his shirt.

"You're hurt," I babbled.

"No, it's Tommy's blood," he tried to say, only his teeth were chattering so much, he could hardly talk. "There's blood all over you, too."

My left arm was throbbing painfully, but other things were more important. "Listen, Vinny," I said urgently, "two cops came to the house looking for you. *Did* you help the Pearls break into Megabytes?"

He was already shaking his head. "The Pearls didn't steal from Megabytes, Mai. Tommy did. He just wanted to do something that'd give him juice so he could join the Pearls. But one of the CKs found out what Tommy'd done and dropped a dime on him to the cops. Tommy just asked me to keep the stuff he took from Megabytes until the heat was off him."

"And you—do you belong to the Pearls yourself?" When he didn't answer, I grabbed hold of him and glared into his eyes. "You answer me, Vinny Tranh, and don't you dare lie to me. Are you mixed up with that gang?"

He shook his head again, and I threatened, "You better not be lying to me. 'Cause if you do belong to the Pearls, I'll—I'll—"

"I *don't* belong to them, Mai. I swear! I came here because the Pearls were going to get even with the CKs that ratted Tommy out. Sammy let me come 'cause I'm Tommy's friend, and now I think they've killed him—"

Then Vinny quit talking and pulled away from me to sink his head on Tommy Vuong's bloody chest, and I wrapped my arms around Vinny, and both of us bawled like babies.

Chapter Ten

LATER WE FOUND out that someone in one of the houses, shut and barred to me, had called 911. Police cordoned off the area and paramedics rushed Tommy Vuong into the ambulance. "I want to go with him," Vinny begged, and when the policemen tried to question him about the shooting, all he could say was "Tommy's dying, isn't he? Please don't let Tommy die."

Vinny was soaked with Tommy's blood and mine. Both of us were such a mess that the paramedics told the cops they could question us at Brighton Hospital. They then bundled Vinny and me into the ambulance along with Tommy. On our way I heard them radio ahead that they had one, and possibly two more gunshot victims, apparently shot with low-velocity weapons.

The triage team was waiting for us when we got to Brighton Hospital. Tommy was raced into surgery; Vinny and I got split up. In the trauma room where I was taken, I was stripped down and examined all over. "How many shots did you hear, honey?" one of the nurses kept asking me. "Did you feel anything that hurt—besides your left arm, I mean?"

Numb, scared out of my ever-loving mind and standing there without a stitch of clothes on, I shook my head. "We have to make sure you're not wounded someplace else," the nurse explained. She gave me a motherly pat and added, "Sometimes, in the panic of the moment, people don't realize they've been shot. But you'll be fine, hon. Just as soon as we get this arm tended to."

They put a hospital jonny on me, wrapped me in a blanket to stop my shaking, and worked on my arm. A young doctor by the name of Parsad came in, read my chart, checked me out, and ordered X rays of my arm. "So we are sure there is no bone involvement," he said. "Otherwise, it seems like a fairly straightforward case. Just through-and-through, yes? We will start an IV to replace fluids, nurse, and we will also need antibiotics and a tetanus shot right away."

He asked me what had happened, and I tried to tell him even though I'd started to shake and my stomach hurt big-time. I was explaining that the CKs had been following me, when two police officers came in the room and asked to talk to me.

So I went through it all again. I'd been out walking on Park Vale near Ringe Street, I said, and been chased by some CKs. While I was running away from them, I'd spotted my cousin Vinny in a car with some other people who turned out to be members of the Pearl gang. Then the Pearls and CKs had opened fire on each other and Vinny and I were caught in the middle.

"Is your cousin Vinh a member of the Pearls?" one of the officers then asked. I said no, he wasn't, that he was just Tommy's friend.

I asked how Tommy was, but nobody could tell me, and after the officers had asked their questions and gone, I thought about him. That lowlife Sammy Vuong had left his kid brother lying in the street and taken off with his friends. If it had been David lying there, I wouldn't have left him—no, not even if a hundred CKs were after me.

Suddenly, I wanted my folks. It didn't matter anymore if they were mad at me or not, if they wanted me or not, *I* wanted my pint-size, red-haired mom to put her arms around me and tell me everything would be okay, baby, and not just with me but with Tommy, too. I wanted my dad standing there as big as life and ready to take on any gang that had *dared* to hurt his little girl. I needed Liz to talk to—she could be a dweeb sometimes, but my sister'd never, ever have turned on me as Nancy had tonight. And David—I was feeling so low that even David would've looked good to me right then.

If a nurse hadn't walked in just then to take me down to X ray, I'd have broken down and bawled. As it was, I had no time for tears because at X ray Vinny, Lien, and Diep were waiting.

Vinny looked a bloody mess—literally. Blood had soaked through his shirt and pants and dripped onto his sneakers, and the few people in X ray edged away from him as he ran up to me and asked if I was okay. "You aren't hurt bad, huh, Mai?" he pleaded.

He looked so scared, I tried to make a joke and said all I had was a through-and-through. "I kept asking about Tommy, but nobody knows," Vinny then muttered. "Jeeze, he might die. Jeez."

He began to cry. Diep kept a hand on Vinny's shoulder and kept on patting him. Lien meanwhile eyed me uncertainly. "Vinh say you save his life," she said. "He say that you get shot because of him."

She looked older than I'd ever seen her. *Beaten* wasn't a word I'd ever have used to describe Lien Van Tranh, but tonight she looked as if she'd been through the wringer. "It wasn't Vinny's fault," I said. "We just got caught in a shootout between the Pearls and the CKs."

Nobody asked me any more questions until I'd been X-rayed and taken back to a waiting area. Here Dr. Parsad came to report that there seemed to be no bone involvement. "Even so, we're going to keep Mai overnight for observation," he told Lien and Diep. "We want to be sure her circulation, sensation, and motion are all right."

"What that mean?" Lien demanded. She listened intently as Dr. Parsad explained that sometimes the swelling that followed a bullet wound in the arm could compress nerves and blood vessels in the arm and hand. "Okay," she then said, "you keep niece. I stay here, too."

The doctor, who looked too tired to deal with a mean-looking Asian lady, ignored her. "How do you feel?" he asked me.

I said fine, which wasn't quite accurate. I felt cold to the marrow of my bones, and my head was throbbing. When I got up from the chair in the waiting room, I felt the room spin a cartwheel.

Dr. Parsad steadied me, told me to stay put for a few minutes until the wooziness passed, and walked out. Lien said, "You don't look too good." Extending her hand, she felt my forehead. "You got fever."

"I'm okay," I muttered.

"Okay, shmokay," announced my aunt. "I going call Dr. Sayel."

Shooing Diep and Vinny ahead of her, she started to leave the room, but then turned back abruptly. "What happened tonight, ha?"

A little surprised, I started to repeat what I'd said earlier about being caught in a crossfire between the Pearls and the CKs. "No, earlier. At restaurant. Nguyen say you disgrace family by telling lies about Vinh to police. Vinh tell me that Nguyen is the one who tell lies. He say you never steal stuff from electronics store." I nodded silent agreement, and she added, "My son say that he agree to hide stolen stuff for Tommy Vuong. He say you saw this happening." She folded her arms across her chest and stared at me as if hoping I would say it wasn't so. "Is true?"

"Yes," I said. "It's true. Nancy thought I snitched on Vinny. I tried to lie like she wanted me to, but I guess I'm not a good liar. The police didn't believe me."

Abruptly Lien went out and left me alone with my chills and dizziness, which got so bad I had to lie down and close my eyes. I felt so sick that I didn't open them again even when I heard Dr. Parsad saying, "Fever and chills—possibly a result of shock. Get this child to bed, nurse."

I threw up while they were getting me onto a gurney and felt royally miserable as I was being wheeled down the corridor toward the elevators. There, Lien caught up with us. "Where you take niece?" she demanded. When told she added, "I stay with her tonight."

The nurse with me said that was against hospital policy and that they'd take care of me. "You can come see her tomorrow," she added.

Lien was unhappy about leaving me. She asked about a hundred questions and demanded to see where I'd be staying. "Tomorrow I come early, make sure you doing okay. I phone to Dr. Sayel, but she not home. I try again soon." She paused a beat and then added, "You, nurse, make sure you take care of this girl. Ha? You don't, you be sorry."

I opened one eye and saw a double image of Lien glaring at the nurse. I shut it quickly and heard her footsteps walk away. "Some people like to make trouble," sniffed the nurse.

I felt like shouting—that woman's had more trouble than you'll ever dream about. She's faced up to bombs and starvation and death, so what's a little hospital red tape? And then I realized that for the first time since I'd known her, I wanted to stick up for Lien. But then, this was the first time Lien was actually on my side.

Apparently my fever spiked during the night, because people kept popping up next to my bed. They fed me antibiotics intravenously and kept waking me up to check my temperature and blood pressure, but I didn't pay much attention to any of it because I felt so miserable. I was pretty much out of it until I heard a familiar voice call my name.

"It's two A.M.," Dr. Sayel replied when I asked her what time it was. "Your aunt finally reached me, and I came to check up on you."

I said I felt awful. "What's the matter with me?" I moaned. "Blood poisoning or gangrene, or what?"

"You've been seeing too many doctor movies." As she spoke, Dr. Sayel was checking me over, and I felt the strong, reassuring touch of her hands. "Want to

151

hear my diagnosis? You have a combination of the bullet that passed through the fleshy part of your arm and a dose of that intestinal flu that's been going around."

She added that neither was dangerous nor fatal. I asked her about Tommy Vuong, and her smile slid away as she said that Tommy was listed in critical condition.

"It's too close to call—we'll have to hope he's tough enough to pull out of this." She pushed back the hair from my forehead and smiled down at me. "Go back to sleep, Mai. Don't take any wooden bullets."

I tried to come up with some snappy retort, but my mouth felt like refrigerator mold and my head was acting like a rivet gun, so I just shut my eyes and went to sleep. In the dreams that followed, I thought I could hear someone humming a haunting, wordless song nearby.

When I managed to open my eyes, it was daylight and Jon was sitting on the chair beside my bed reading a magazine. A balloon that said "Hope You Have a Good Day" bobbled in the air above him.

I must have moved, because he looked up, saw me, and the worried look in his eyes eased away. "Look who woke up finally," he said. I croaked a question, and he said, "Doc Sayel called to tell me you'd been hurt, so I came by before work. For crying out loud, Iowa, don't you know better than to walk into a gang shootout?"

His eyes were warm and blue and smiling, and he looked good even though there seemed two of him weaving and bobbing in front of me. "I forgot to duck," I mumbled tiredly.

He pulled the chair closer to me and awkwardly patted my hand. After a few minutes he said, "I heard Tommy Vuong wasn't so lucky. He's still in the ICU."

"What about Sammy?" I asked.

"He's disappeared." The look on Jon's face told me what he thought of Sammy Vuong. "But there's good news, too. Hector's doing fine at Gorham Rehab, and he may be able to move out of there soon."

I was about to ask him where could Hector possibly go to, when Lien walked in. She gave Jon a cold stare and stayed standing until he said he'd see me later.

"That the Ireland boy who is boyfriend to you?" she demanded as soon as he'd left the room. I said that Jon and I were friends from the clinic. "How good friends?" she persisted.

Too sick for a debate with my aunt, I closed my eyes. She didn't say anything more, but I could hear paper rustling. "I bring some things from restaurant," she explained. "Hospital food always very bad."

I opened one eye and saw that the windowsill was now covered with stuff—a basket of fruit, dishes of shrimp, steamed rice, spareribs, and, of course, Grandma Bach Thi's spring rolls. "Everybody want send something," Lien explained. "Diep cook steamed rice with coconut cream for you. Vinh and Luu make the spring rolls. And this fruit from Cousin Gian. He want come with me, but I say you don't feel too good yet."

"Thanks," I croaked. I appreciated the thought, but the sight of food made me sick, so I closed my eyes again. "How's Gian making out?" I asked.

"He helping at restaurant," my aunt said, as if this were the most natural thing in the world. Then she added somberly, "Diep and me, we go to the police this morning with Vinh. Lucky for him, he not really mixed up with gang, just hang around with his friend Tommy. Officers, they yell at Vinh and scare him good. Then they ask many questions to us about Jade Palace restaurant and how the Pearls are always helping them."

Lien paused a beat and then added, "I ask Vinh why he want to join with gang. I say, you have everything you need—food, house, school, family. What more you need?"

True bewilderment rode her voice. Too sick to be

diplomatic, I blurted out, "You're so hard on him. You make him and Nancy work all the time—"

I broke off, remembering how Nancy had turned on me. "You have to ease up on Vinny," I finished somewhat lamely.

"Have to work to live," Lien bristled.

"But you have to *live*, too," I pointed out. Even with my eyes tightly closed I could sense Lien frowning at me, but the way I felt, I didn't care whether or not I made her mad. "You could have let Vinny have the video games he wanted. He's such a good kid, works so hard. It's like you always have to be the boss of everybody. It's unfair."

"It's life. Life not fair."

"I know, but—"

"You know nothing," she snapped. "You think 'hard' mean a bad mark at school or maybe you fight with friend or be punished, ha? I know better than you. So I work, make family strong, so they survive."

I opened my eyes and saw her sitting bolt upright in the chair by my bed, a short, lean, hard-faced lady with burning, defiant eyes.

"I lose too many of my family already," she told me. "Las' night I almost lose Vinh."

The pain in my head and the stuff they were giving me for my stomach was making me sleepy. But as I closed my eyes again, she added, "Like I lose your ma, my sister."

This was what I'd been hoping for, the day when Lien would open up to me and talk about Mai Hongvan. This was why I'd come to Boston. Go figure—now that Lien was finally ready to talk, my head felt like a concrete mixer, and I had to fight to keep my eyes open.

"Mai was the youngest sister in family," she was saying. "I was the oldest. Mai was six year younger than me. When she was baby, I took care of her—always, I take good care of her."

"What did she look like?"

My voice sounded slurred, even to me. Maybe because of the medication or perhaps because of the flu, I felt as if I were floating, as if while my body was on that hospital bed, my mind could run free and slide between reality and dreams. I know it sounds weird, but as Lien spoke about Mai Hongvan, it seemed almost as if I were there *with* her, seeing what she described.

Baby Mai Hongvan, tiny like Nancy, with Nancy's dark hair, dances through a green field picking flowers with chubby fingers. She brings the flowers to her big sister. Lien, about ten years old and smiling, combs her sister's black hair and sings to her, and it seems to me that I am listening to the tuneless, haunting melody I've heard in my dreams.

I blinked open my eyes and saw that Lien—two Liens, actually—was sitting in the chair by my hospital bed. The wordless song in my mind seemed to fade as she said, "She was always pretty, like doll. When Mai was sixteen, all the boys in the village and from the next village, too, fell in love with her. Want to marry her." She added contemptuously, "Even that old turtle Cao Vuong was in love with my sister."

I remembered the way Mr. Vuong had spoken of Mai Hongvan. "Did she like Mr. Vuong?" I asked.

"Like everybody as friend, nobody in special way. Mai is very tender-hearted. Don't want any boy to suffer or feel sad. So she don't choose any boy at all." Lien's lips tugged in an almost-smile as she added, "Our parents want Mai to marry, but she don't want a husband yet. So I tell them, don't force her. I tell them, Mai is still young, must be happy with the husband she chooses. Parents listened to me, and Mai was free."

Free and happy, Mai Hongvan stands flying a kite from a green mountaintop. Near her, Lien nurses her small son, Khi. The wind blows off Mai's straw hat, and she laughs merrily and catches it—

The image blurred, swirled in my dizzy brain. "She's delirious," I heard a nurse say. "The fever keeps spiking."

I felt sorry for that nurse. She didn't realize that I was watching a slender girl with long black hair flying her kite on a mountaintop. *Mai*, I called—or tried to call, and she turned around and looked at me, and I saw my own face smiling at me.

"She was so gentle," Lien was saying, and her harsh voice drew me down from the green mountaintop and back into my hospital bed. "Too gentle for life, my little sister. Should have married nice neighbor boy, had babies, lived happy." She paused on a new thought. "We *were* happy in that time. People hear Vietnam and say, 'Oh, that is the place where there was war,' but once our village was beautiful."

In the small village near Bao Loc, the elderly man whose face I saw once in Lien's black-and-white photograph and his son-in-law, Diep, make fishing nets and cast them into water that reflects the blue sky. The old lady and her three daughters tend crops on the family's small vegetable farm. Coffee plants spread their thick, starry blossoms near the thatch-roofed house and fill the air with their scent.

Time passes. Ha Thi marries and moves away. But then Diep's older brother is killed fighting the Viet Cong, and the war draws near, and the old man, the old lady, and the young people are sobbing because their village is burning from firebombs, and they must leave.

"We walk long time, finally reach big town," I heard Lien say, and I was back again in the hospital and far from the smoke and the fire and the tears. "No money, no work—too many refugees, all running from war. We are hungry—very hungry—all the time. My son Khi is so sick. There is no food. Diep finds work helping Americans as laborer, but he is hurt in back and cannot move. I try find work as servant, but cannot find. Then Mai find only work she can get."

There was a small pause, and then Lien added, "With this money we buy food, medicine. We can eat, and Khi gets better."

"Where—where did she work?" I whispered.

"In a bar. She say, 'All this time, my family take care of me. Now I take care of my family.'" There was another heartbeat's silence before Lien added, "But she *work* only at bar. She don't have American boyfriends. All of them want her to go with them, but she say no. Each night after work, Diep go and wait for her, bring her home."

"Then who—" I began, but Lien cut me short. All work ended, she said, when the American forces left Vietnam in 1973.

"But we have to stay and live under the Communists. Bad years come, very bad. The Communists take my father away to reeducation camp. They think he has sympathy with Americans. Father die in camp. Mother get sick in the heart and she die, too." Lien drew a deep breath and added, "Nguyen is born in this bad time."

Two months after Nancy was born, the family learned that Diep, still half-crippled from his back injury—was to be sent away to the reeducation camp. "We know he die there, too," Lien told me. "None of us can do nothing."

I can see the family in terror. Mai Hongvan holds baby Nancy in her arms and rests her cheek against the baby's fuzz of hair. She is very quiet—I know she's thinking that there must be a way to save the family.

"Only way is to leave Vietnam," Lien was saying, "but this not easy. In our town people with boats have been caught trying to escape. They are punished; many killed. People are afraid to try and escape. But there was one man who wasn't afraid."

Diep had heard of the American who operated out of Malaysia. A GI during the war, he was now a profiteer who made a good living ferrying desperate refugees out of Vietnam to Hong Kong.

"That man wanted much money; we not have money," Lien said starkly. "No use to even hope. But when we hear that the American is going to be take another ship full of refugees from a place near our town, my sister Mai have idea. She took what money we have and bribed the American's contacts in our town. They arrange for her to meet with American so she could beg him to take us."

Mai Hongvan, slender in her flowing white ao-dai *and black pants, a white flower tucked into her shining hair, goes to meet the captain of the boat. She puts her palms together and bows deeply before him, bows almost to the floor. She pleads with him: Please, she says, save my family. I'll do anything you wish if you save my family.*

I could almost hear her say the words—I could definitely picture her standing there, pleading with the profiteer. Her desperation was so real that it hurt me. "Did he take you?" I whispered, and Lien nodded. Yes.

Then she added, "My sister was beautiful, beautiful girl. No man would say no to her—not even the boat captain."

Still to come were the horrors of the journey—the storms, the hunger, little Khi catching a cold that turned swiftly to pneumonia. Khi dying. His burial at sea. Mai, pale as death herself, holding Lien back when she wanted to jump into the water after her son. "My sister Mai tells me that I must think of Nguyen," Lien grated. "She says I must not die."

She sounded angry, and she *looked* angry, too—more so than I'd ever seen her. I knew I risked channeling that anger toward me, but I had to know. "Was that boat captain my father?" She nodded, wordless. "Is that why you tore up all the photographs of Mai Hongvan? Why you never talked about her?"

All red in the face, Lien snapped, "You don't know nothing. You better keep quiet now."

But I'd had it with keeping quiet. Disregarding the pounding in my head, I propped myself up on an arm and glared at Lien. "She saved your lives, damn it," I cried. "Why should you hate her for that?"

"Not hate her," Lien said. "Not hate *her*—"

Her voice cracked on the word, and she bit her lip.

158

Tears filled her eyes and began to overflow onto her hard, brown cheeks. As I stared in total shock, she whispered, "I hate myself. Myself! I could not save her. Could not take care of her. My baby sister—"

More tears were rolling down Lien's cheeks. She didn't even try to wipe them away, and her voice, raw and harsh and clipped, mourned, "Mai not carry her baby easy. She became so sick in the refugee camp. Diep and I, we try to find medicine, best food. Mai cannot eat. I hold her in my arms, tell her, 'You must get well. We will all go to America and have a good life,' I tell her. She smiled at me—"

Lien drew a deep, shaky breath, pulled off her glasses, and mopped her eyes with her arm. "When she die, I cannot think of her. Cannot bear speak her name. Cannot even see photograph of Mai. If I think of my sister, I don't want to live no more. All the time I am desperate to die and end the pain—but Nguyen need me. For her I must live. That is what Mai told me."

She broke off and whispered, "She was too gentle for life. My baby sister."

I was crying along with Lien. Not just for Mai Hongvan, who'd had so much love in her heart, given so much, and gotten so little back, but also for the pain I saw in Lien's eyes, heard in Lien's voice. For everything she'd kept buried until I showed up on her doorstep.

"Why didn't you tell me not to come?" I asked, and she shrugged.

"At first I don't want you come. I hide your letter, tried to forget. But I cannot forget about Mai. You are her child, and—"

Lien broke off abruptly and got to her feet. "No use talking," she said wearily. "Talking don't change anything."

Then she walked out of the room. Exhausted from crying, from fever, from learning too much too quickly, I slept. When I woke up again, there was still a dull ache in my head, but the dizziness was gone. I felt cooler, and my stomach had quit doing flipflops.

Dr. Sayel came in a second after I'd opened my eyes. "You're all better," she said after she checked me out. "In fact, it's my professional opinion that you'll live."

"Where's Lien?" I asked. "And what time is it?"

It was late afternoon, Dr. Sayel said, and she'd met Lien in the corridor and sent her down to the cafeteria to get a bite. "She looked pretty peaked actually," she went on, "and no wonder. She's been with you all day."

"I know," I said.

"Don't worry—she's as tough as nails, your aunt. She always was since the early days, when I first got to know her." The doctor looked thoughtful. "I wouldn't want to go against that lady, but in a tight spot I'd definitely want her at my back. The nurses say that she watched over you like a tigress defending its cub."

This, too, I knew. What she'd told me had made me realize why Lien, who'd not been able to save Mai Hongvan, would fight, tooth and nail, to protect her own.

With what Lien had told me, I could fit most of the pieces into my own personal puzzle. The picture was almost complete, except for one missing piece. It was a biggie. I hadn't asked Lien, and she hadn't told me, whether—

But that thought was interrupted by the sound of voices coming down the corridor. Then the door burst open, and I stared at the four redheaded people framed in the doorway.

"Oh, my *Lord*," Mom gasped. "what have they *done* to you, baby?"

Chapter Eleven

MOM RAN ACROSS the room, practically mashing me in a hug. I yelped with pain as the IV was almost yanked out of my arm, but being mashed felt so great! Dad hugged me next, and I'd definitely have started bawling if I hadn't just then gotten a good look at my kid brother.

"What happened to *you*?" I gasped.

David's hair had been shaved off except for this carroty tuft on top of his head. At the nape of his neck was a pathetic braid of hair that looked like a starved-mouse's tail. Together with the cast that covered his leg from ankle to the knee and his too-big purple T-shirt, he looked like something out of the late-night Creature Feature.

"It's the latest craze," Mom said in a resigned voice. Then she added anxiously, "Baby, are you sure you're all right?"

I truly felt fine—now. "You should see the other guy," I joked.

David and I grinned at each other, and Liz said, "You don't know what happened when we got that call from Mrs. Tranh this morning. I mean, we *moved*."

"She should have phoned us when it happened last night," Dad rumbled. He started to get all red in the face as he added, "I want to know what the police are doing about this."

Just then Lien walked into the room. "Are you Mrs. Tranh?" Dad boomed.

He gave her a once-over through narrowed eyes.

Not to be intimidated, Lien stuck out her chin. "You Leo Houston, ha?"

"I didn't send my daughter to Boston so she could be shot at by criminals," Dad started to say, when Mom, the peacemaker, interrupted.

"We're just shocked at seeing our daughter in the hospital, Mrs. Tranh."

"I was shocked, too," Lien came back. She folded her arms across her chest and stuck out her chin farther. "I didn't want phone you in middle of night. What you can do then except worry? So I wait till this morning."

She and my father eyed each other, suspicious and taking each other's measure. It was a sight to see— Houston versus Tranh.

Dr. Sayel introduced herself then and said I was doing fine. "Mai had to deal with a gunshot wound in her left arm and a touch of the meanest intestinal flu that's hit us in a decade," she said. "Nothing to worry about, however, I assure you."

Even my dad couldn't resist Dr. Sayel's smile. I could see him starting to melt, and he sounded quite mellow as he shook hands and thanked her for taking care of me. Mom kept patting me the way Diep had patted Vinny last night.

"I wish I'd come with you to Boston, baby. I should have called you and written to you more. I *wanted* to," she added with an accusing look at Dad, "but your father talked me out of it."

Dad cleared his throat. "Your mother and I agreed that it would be better if we gave you some space, Mai."

Mom patted me again and then moved off to talk to Dr. Sayel, and Liz came to perch on my bed. "You look so thin," she said enviously. "I gained five pounds at camp—it was really boring this year. I kept wondering how you were doing."

Meaning that she'd missed me. I got a lump in my throat. I'd known I was homesick before this, but I'd never guessed how much until they all came through the door. "I missed you guys," I said.

Liz then surprised the heck out of me by throwing her arms around me and hugging me. I hugged back, feeling an ache of tears behind my eyes. "At least you got away from David," Liz said, laughing to cover up.

Our kid brother was hopping around on his cast and crutches, poking at all the machines in the room. "You be careful, boy," Lien directed sternly. To my father she added, "You don't have to worry. I watch out for Mai. Call Dr. Sayel, make sure nurses at this hospital do right things for niece."

My father said he'd like to thank the people who'd taken care of me, and Dr. Sayel said she'd introduce him to Dr. Parsad. She started to follow my dad out of the room and then paused.

"Mai has been a blessing to have around the center," she told Mom. "She has a special empathy with patients that's very rare." Then she smiled at me and said, "We could use someone like you in the health care profession, Mai."

I could see Mom's eyes light up: my daughter, the doctor. For a second she basked in that thought, and then she sobered. "How did Mai come to be shot?" she asked Lien.

"Because of my son." Brutally frank as always, she added, "Vinh think he want to join the Pearl gang. Mai was caught in fight between Pearls and CKs."

"Vinh's a *gang* member?" David asked, delighted and impressed. "Awesome!"

Lien regarded my brother with a frown. "Not awesome at all. Stupid boys shooting each other." Then she remembered her manners and gave my mom a little formal bow. "Later, please you come eat at restaurant, and we talk."

"We're looking forward to meeting your family," Mom replied, equally polite. "Mai has told us so much about her cousins."

Lien just nodded without speaking, and I suddenly

163

realized that in all this time Nancy's name hadn't come up once.

My cousin Nancy, my once good friend—was she still mad at me? Actually, I told myself, it should be the other way around because she'd gotten me into all kinds of trouble. I'd been hurt by her, furious with her, but at least now I understood what family meant to the Tranhs, that Nancy would have done anything to keep Vinny out of trouble, and I hadn't measured up according to her lights. On top of that I'd showed her up as a liar, so she wasn't about to forgive me in a hurry.

I hoped she'd come to the hospital and that we could make peace, but only Vinny stopped by that evening with Uncle Diep. He was real pale and quiet, and I figured that he'd been scared silly at the police station, until David piped up with, "Did you guys *really* get caught in a gang shootout?"

Vinny looked sick. Diep said, "Tommy Vuong die this afternoon."

Everybody went totally still. Diep went on. "It is so stupid. Not fair. Tommy was only fourteen—"

Vinny made a choking sound and bolted out of the room. Diep started to go after him, then paused to say, "Vuong family lose two sons. Tommy is dead. Sammy is criminal, wanted by police." His eyes filled with tears as he added, "Vuongs were such good parents. So good, so kind. Why do they deserve this?"

I didn't know what to say. Looking ready to cry herself, Mom went over to Diep and patted his arm. "Kids," she sighed. "All we can do is love them—and then sometimes it isn't enough."

That evening Jon came to see me again. He brought me cookies from his mother and a bunch of flowers that made Liz roll her eyes at me and suck her braces in her disgusting way.

"I've got good news," he told me after he'd gotten introduced all around and Dad had asked the obligatory father questions like what school do you go to, and what sports do you play, and where do you intend to go to college? "Like I almost said this morning, Hector's going home."

"But how can he?" I asked, bewildered. "Can he take care of himself?"

"The Family Group has it covered." Jon then explained that Judy's Wednesday group had held a special meeting and decided that they would split shifts and take care of Hector around the clock. "It's their way of thanking him for all those veggies and flowers he used to bring," Jon went on. "Judy said they voted unanimously to help out for as long as it takes."

I'd already clued my family in about the center, so they knew about the Family Group and Judy and, naturally, about Mr. Gonsalves. Dad cleared his throat and pointed out that human nature being what it was, the Family Group might start out with good intentions and then run out of steam.

"If they ever do, Judy will fire them up again," Jon said. "Anyway, they'll have a lot of help. Nate said he'd sleep over Hector's the first week he was home, and my dad and me are ready to take the next week if we're needed. Besides which, Hector's neighbors have made up a roster of who's going to drive him to therapy and who'll help him take care of Bolivar."

I said, he had to be dreaming. "No one would ever get close to the cat from hell."

"Believe it or not, the old boy's mellowing out," Jon said. "He even let me pat him today, though I didn't like the way he sniffed my hand—it was sort of like he wanted to check me out before biting me."

Then he added, "Hector's been asking about you, and I said you'd come see him soon. When are you getting out of here?"

The hospital sprang me next morning, Tuesday, and I went to stay with my folks in their hotel. Lien had agreed that this was best. "Hotel has room service," she said, and added in a rare attempt at humor, "You got shot; now you *big*shot."

But she looked relieved, and I guessed that she was glad to avoid a confrontation between me and Nancy. I'd asked about my cousin, but from the vague way everybody answered my questions, I gathered that Nancy was still mad at me. It bothered me, but there didn't seem much I could do about it besides confronting her—and I wasn't ready for that.

At first the folks wanted to get back to Iowa by midweek, but Liz and David said that wasn't fair. Since I wasn't dying or anything, they wanted to see Boston. Upon hearing this, Mom confessed that she'd like to shop the big stores at Copley Square and, by the way, what about those great outlet stores in Kittery, Maine?

Dad held out muttering about having to get back to work until he met the Delaneys, who dropped by the hotel on Tuesday night with Jon. Mrs. D. and Mom hit if off right away, and Mr. D. invited the whole family to go on a whale watch on the *Alba Anne*. Against my advice, Dad accepted for the whole family.

I said, no way was I ever going to go on another whale watch, and that instead I'd go visit Mr. Gonsalves and maybe stop in at the clinic. Mom, who thought the world of Dr. Sayel, said this was a good idea. "Lien has been asking us to come to the Spring Restaurant," she added, "so we'll all meet there for dinner."

Jon had split up his Wednesday work schedule, getting off at two so that we could go visit Mr. Gonsalves together. It was a good thing, since I'd never have found Gorham Rehab on my own. First we had to take the T to Park Street, and then hop a streetcar and finally a bus. As we rattled along, I tested my still-sore left arm and realized how used to the big city I'd become. It wasn't possible that I'd be back in Serena in just a couple of days.

"What're you thinking about?" Jon asked.

"Iowa," I told him. "Serena's going to seem *so* small when I go back."

Jon nodded somberly. "I guess," he said. Then he added, "I'll miss you."

"Likewise," I said.

He took hold of my good hand and gave it a squeeze. "The world's a small place. I was flipping through this book of colleges yesterday, and there are a couple of good ones in Iowa."

He gave the hand he was holding a little swing, and I looked up into blue eyes that smiled down into mine in a way that made the dull ache in my arm go away. "There are a few good colleges here in Boston, too," I said deadpan. "Harvard, MIT, Boston University, Boston College. Not many, but a *few*."

We smiled at each other. "The world's a small place," Jon repeated. Then he said, "So small, we just missed our stop."

Though Jon seemed to think that I'd been rendered so feeble by my through-and-through shot that I could hardly put one foot in front of the other, I insisted we walk to the Gorham Rehabilitation Center. This was a huge, imposing brick building with automatic glass doors that shut behind us with a decisive snap. There were people in wheelchairs in the hallways, jonny-clad patients on crutches, and sad-eyed visitors waiting for the elevator, which smelled of antiseptic and medicine. The intercom bleeped continuously, paging doctors.

I was sure that Mr. Gonsalves would hate this place and steeled myself for the worst. When I got to the door of his semiprivate room I pasted a bright smile on my face and stepped smartly through it—into a sea of flowers.

The room was buried in every kind of plant and flower you could think of. There were vases of cosmos, roses, dahlias, and other flowers I didn't even recognize. A bonsai pine tree stood elegantly in a pot; an avocado was sprouting in a jam jar. There was a basin full of water lilies on the floor near the window.

Mr. Gonsalves himself was playing checkers with his roommate. The first thing I noticed was that he didn't look so pale or so shrunken anymore, and the second thing was the way he could *move*. Smiling with pleasure at the sight of us, he grabbed hold of a walker beside him and did a shuffle-limp over to us.

"Ay, you and me, we are twins," he said to me as he hugged us as best he could. "We both have only one good arm."

His roommate, whose bed was also half hidden with flowers, said that Mr. Gonsalves was a card. "Show them how good you can walk, Hec," he added.

So we progressed out of the room and down the corridor, where people called Mr. Gonsalves by name and asked him how he was doing. A pretty nurse with a fresh-cut rose in her hair stopped to tell me how much she'd miss Mr. Gonsalves when he left. "You wouldn't believe the visitors this man gets," she told me. "It's like Fenway Park in there."

Mr. Gonsalves beamed after her. "That is Señorita Jenny," he told us. "She has been so kind to me, so patient." He paused to greet another nurse and then turned his smile on me. "I have never thanked you for helping me that day, Mai. Were it not for you, I would never have lived long enough to come to this so-beautiful place."

He gestured around him, and I marveled. Other people might have tied themselves into knots hating where they were, but Mr. Gonsalves thought it was beautiful.

Still, he was eager to get home and asked a hundred questions. He asked about his garden, his neighbors, and most of all about Bolivar. Then he related proudly that the cat had actually *purred* for one of his neighbors. "He has become civilized, my clever old caballero," he said. "When next you see him, he will eat from your hand."

Somehow, I doubted *that*—but as he spoke, I knew how much I'd miss Mr. Gonsalves.

"I will miss you also," he said as if he'd read my thoughts. "I know you will go away soon, Mai, back to Iowa. Has your quest been completed?"

I sketched out for them what Lien had told me at the hospital. "So now you know a lot more about your birth mother," Jon mused. "Are you happy about it?"

I said it was a mixed bag. "I know a lot more about what happened and why it happened," I said. "But I found out some really bad stuff, too. The guy who— you know, the captain of that refugee boat—I don't like the thought of being related to *him*."

Mr. Gonsalves said we couldn't judge anyone. "Perhaps he was not a bad man after all," he pointed out. "Perhaps he truly loved your mother. We were not there, so we do not know. Besides, you are not Mai Hongvan or this nameless man. You are Mai Houston."

I didn't know what to say. Mr. Gonsalves went on. "We are all human, and so we make mistakes. Look at me, Mai, at this foolish old man who believed himself to be all alone, with no family in this world. Who felt so sorry for himself because he was sure he was going to die lonely and forgotten. Ha!"

He threw up his head and laughed—the first laugh I'd ever heard out of him—a rich, deep, happy sound. "I was mistaken. I was wrong! My friends at the Sayel Center, my neighbors, you and Jon—*you* are my family."

Jon and I stayed with Mr. Gonsalves for another half hour, during which a steady stream of people arrived with more flowers, fruit, and homemade cookies until, by the time we left, a party was going on. "It's good to see the old guy so happy." Jon beamed as we walked out of the rehab center.

The happiness was contagious, so after we'd taken the streetcar back to Brookline Village, we decided to walk.

169

Talking, shoulders bumping, we covered the length of Harvard Avenue as it crossed Brookline and entered Brighton. It was a hike, all right, but I didn't mind. My arm didn't hurt anymore, the afternoon was warm and sunny but not August-hot, and as we walked, I saw a kite bobbing high in the sky.

I told Jon about the morning Vinny and I'd flown his dragon kite and how I should have seen trouble coming. Jon said that I was being foolish. "You're not superwoman, Iowa. How could you have known? Besides, you were there for Vinny when it counted. You could've gotten yourself killed, trying to protect him."

I'd thought about this a lot; I'd even had nightmares about that night. But I also knew that I'd have done it all over again if I had to. "It's been some summer," I sighed.

Lien and the restaurant and Nancy hating me and Vinny's arm cut up, the Pearls and the CKs, poor Tommy Vuong dead at fourteen, and those Orchids living in fear—I thought about it all as we walked down the last leg of Harvard Avenue toward Springvale. So much sadness, so much pain, but in the balance, there was Mr. Gonsalves's newfound joy, Dr. Sayel's warm smile, the center, and Jon—Jon that day on the *Alba Anne* saying, puzzled, "You're Mai Houston."

"You've gotten real quiet," he was saying. "Is your arm hurting?" I said no, and he asked, "When is your plane taking off, Mai?"

I said Friday. "Darn it, I work all day tomorrow *and* Friday. I'll try to get off, but I mightn't even get to see you off."

We stopped where we were—on the corner of Harvard and Springvale—and looked at each other, and I felt a hard lump form in my throat as I realized how much I didn't want to say good-bye.

The by-now-familiar smells of the Korean market surrounded us, and I could hear the music someone was playing down the street, and Peterbilt barking

170

from Megabytes, where, I noted, some other kid was already working. Mr. Singh sure hadn't lost time replacing Tommy. And there across the way was—

"Ohmigosh. The Jade Palace is closed down," I exclaimed.

The big restaurant had a padlock on the door. Papers taped to the door announced that the restaurant was closed until further notice.

Perhaps the INS had caught on to the fact that they were hiring illegal immigrants? If so, I wondered what had happened to the poor Orchids. Jon said that if they *were* illegals, the Orchids were probably in detention right now.

"They'll be deported back to China or wherever," he added. "It's rough, but they had to know the risks before they paid some snake to bring them over here. Anyway, life back there's probably better than being a slave."

A week ago I might have agreed with Jon, but now that I'd heard Lien's story, I knew there were really terrible places in the world. I kept thinking of the way Big Orchid had hovered over her baby that day at the center, the way she'd kept kissing its little hands.

"Whatever happens, the Orchids have each other," Jon said, trying to cheer me up. Then he added, "It's getting to be six o'clock—I'd better be going back to Luigi's."

What did you say when someone had become really close, really a part of your life, and you had to say good-bye? I felt tears swim to my eyes as I searched my brain for some memorable words of wisdom.

"Later," I said.

"Yeah, later," Jon agreed. "It's not good-bye, Iowa. It's a—"

"—small world," we said together, and laughed, and then Jon kissed me.

Right there on Springvale with people walking around us and past us, right near the Siam Video

171

Mart, he kissed me. This time there was no "sort of" about it. I *knew* I'd been kissed.

Warm lips and the faint scent of lime aftershave, tender-rough scrape of cheek, tickle of eyelashes against my cheek—that was Jon. Knowing I'd remember this moment forever, I put my good arm around him and hung on and kissed him back and felt as if Springvale Street and all of Brighton had disappeared into smoke.

"I'll write to you," I muttered against Jon's lips.

"Me, too."

We kissed again. In the middle of that kiss, a familiar gruff voice shouted, "You, over there, Mai, that you?"

Hastily, Jon and I drew away from each other, and I groaned to see Lien standing in the restaurant door. She was shading her eyes with the flat of her hand and squinting toward us. "I have to go," I sighed.

"I know," Jon said. "I'll try to see you off on Friday, Mai."

Then he went loping around the corner onto Harvard, leaving me to head for the restaurant. I braced myself for some kind of lecture, but all Lien said was "You too early for dinner. Houstons and Delaneys not here yet."

She held the restaurant door open for me. "You arm feel better now?" she asked. I said it did. "That good. Vinh worry, ask me to ask you."

"Vinny's not here?" I asked, and she shook her head.

That was surprising, especially since the Spring Restaurant seemed busier than I'd ever seen it. "We do good business now," Lien agreed smugly, reading the look in my eyes. She bent closer to add, "That Jade Palace, it have big trouble."

"Immigration?" I hazarded, and she nodded.

"INS people been watching that bad place for hiring illegals people. Ha! Two hours ago officials come,

172

close Jade Palace. Not good to break laws in United States."

Lien looked virtuous and smug. "What did the INS do with the illegal workers?" I asked.

But Lien said that the INS had found no illegal immigrants. "Just before immigration people come, big van come, park in back of that restaurant. I think van take all illegal people away, hide them. Then they sell them again to someone else." She paused to add, "Even so, Jade Palace is in big trouble, you bet."

As she spoke, a slender guy with a Beatles' haircut and horn-rimmed glasses came through the door. He balanced an enormous tray on one shoulder and fielded the swinging door like a pro. "Cousin Gian Cu," Lien announced proudly.

Cousin Gian Cu did a double-take when he recognized me. I couldn't blame him—last time he'd seen me, I was lying on the floor with Nancy pulling out tufts of my hair.

"Hi," I said.

"Hello," he said shyly, and he gave me a bashful smile as he went past with his tray of plates. He wasn't at all like Pham, I thought. At least I'd helped bring over a family member who seemed like a decent human being.

"Where *is* Vinny?" I asked. Lien said, working. "In the kitchen, you mean?" I asked.

"No," she went, "at Megabytes. He work for Mr. Singh."

"For *Mr. Singh*?" I gasped. She gave me a look that clearly said she was impatient with my slowness.

"After that business with police, I go with Vinh to see Mr. Singh," she informed me. "I say, here is a boy who is good boy, but who made mistake and caused you loss of electronics goods. I say, Vinh want to take that poor Tommy Vuong's place, work for two, maybe three hours each afternoon. Work for free till his debt to you is paid."

She paused, and a small smile of satisfaction touched her hard lips. "Mr. Singh impressed with what I say. He say, okay, we'll see how Vinh works out. After that, he say, it's up to Vinh. I think Mr. Singh will like him, will let him work for a few hours each day after school."

She paused. "You right about one thing. Boys need pocket money to buy what they want. I won't give Vinh money, won't spoil my son like old man Vuong. He got to work for what he wants."

Way to go, Vinny—but before that thought could root in my mind, the swinging doors parted and Nancy came through them.

"Ma. Luu needs to know—" she began to say, then broke off as she saw me. A flash of pure hate flared in her eyes, and without another word she turned and walked back through the swinging doors.

I followed her. Nancy wasn't in the kitchen, but the back kitchen door was quivering, as if it had just been slammed. "Look what the cat dragged in," Pham exclaimed.

He was helping Uncle Diep fry ribs. Apparently he'd been promoted from chopping, but this had done nothing for his disposition. He looked more sour than I'd ever seen as he added, "You look like hell."

"Nice to see you, too," I said. Beside Pham, Uncle Diep smiled and nodded at me, and Luu looked up from fixing spring rolls to show her gold tooth in a welcoming grin.

"Where's Nancy?" I asked.

Pham pursed his lips as if tasting something real sweet, and left his smoking pot to sidle over to me. "Our little Nance's in re-eal trouble," he drawled. "When the Woman of Steel heard about Nancy's Japanese boyfriend, she got grounded for a million years. Thanks to you, of course."

I went out the door with Pham's snide remarks still in my ears, out into the small hall and then through the green door. On the steps where she and

I had sat so many evenings this summer, Nancy was smoking.

"Listen," I said. She ignored me. "We have to talk," I persisted.

Nancy drew in smoke and let it slide out into the hot, early-evening air. She watched it go and continued to ignore me. "We need to talk about what happened the other night," I repeated.

"I thought you'd gone back to Iowa." She spat out the words with such scorn that I started feeling angry myself. "You should never have come to see us. We were doing fine without you. Now look what you've done to me."

"You did it to yourself," I cried. "You were the one who lied to Dr. Sayel and your mom—and to me, too. You should've known your lies'd catch up to you someday."

Nancy turned so quickly to face me that her hair whirled around her face like a witch's mane. "Oh, sure. Like you're the big heroine, the one with all the answers. Thanks to you," she went on bitterly, "I can't see Ken. I can't go anywhere except work at this damned restaurant. That's how much my precious mother trusts me now. Maybe she figures I'll be a slut like my dear aunt Mai."

"Don't talk about her like that," I cried.

"Why not, when it's the truth? You think you're so damned smart," she sneered, "coming from Iowa to find out about your roots. Well, your roots aren't so glamorous or pretty, are they? So you'd better go back where you come from. None of us wants you."

Nancy tossed her cigarette away, got up, and elbowed past me into the restaurant. I felt sick and hollow, as if somebody had burned away everything inside of me, leaving only the shell.

Okay, Mai, I asked myself, now what do you do?

Did I face trouble and walk back into the restaurant with my head held high? That would show Nancy I didn't care, that she hadn't hurt me as she'd wanted to, but I couldn't do it. Walk past that sneer-

175

ing Pham—no. I decided instead to go to the center and stay there awhile.

At the center I could lick my wounds, wait for the sting of Nancy's words to grow bearable. It was still early, and I'd have time to get back here in time for dinner with the Delaneys.

So for the second time that day I walked up Harvard and took the streetcar to Union Square. It was past six—technically, the Sayel Center medical hours were over—but if I knew Dr. Sayel, she'd still be there seeing patients. Besides, it was Wednesday night, which meant that there'd be the Family Group meeting in Judy's office.

Union Square was full of kids, but nobody bothered me as I walked toward the center. I tried to keep my mind closed to the hurtful things Nancy had said and tried, instead, to concentrate on how Jon had kissed me—

My thoughts broke off as a rustling noise came from behind the bushes that formed the back border of the garden Mr. Gonsalves had planted for the center. I stopped in my tracks and demanded, "Who's there?" *Rustle, rustle.* "It's not funny," I snapped nervously. "Come out right now!"

Suddenly, there was this wailing sound. *Bolivar*, I thought. Of course, it had to be Bolivar. Judy had said that the cat had gotten lonely and wandered down to the center, looking for Mr. Gonsalves.

"Hey, Bolivar," I started to say, when the wail came again, and this time I *knew* it hadn't come from any cat. I walked around the garden to the bushes, pushed them apart, and stared.

There at my feet, wrapped nose to toes in a soiled sheet, was a squirming, crying baby. Hurriedly, I knelt to push the sheet aside and saw a small round face, tufts of downy dark hair, and a rosebud mouth that now twisted into a wail.

It was Baby Orchid.

Chapter Twelve

BABY ORCHID WAILED and kicked her legs against the sheet. Then she jammed her whole fist into her mouth. Her entire body jerked with frantic sucking.

She was starving. Clutching her to me, I ran through Mr. Gonsalves's garden and up the stairs. Mrs. Menzies had gone home, so I sped past the empty reception area and down the hall. Dr. Sayel wasn't in her office, so I pounded on the door of her consultation room.

"Just a minute, I'm with a patient," the doctor called.

As I stood in the hall, jiggling Baby Orchid in my arms, Judy came out of her office. I told her I'd found Baby Orchid. "I wonder what happened to the mother," she said.

"That's easy—she dumped her kid and took off," Judy's Family Group had followed Judy out of her office into the hall.

Baby Orchid let go of her useless fist and came out with a scream of hunger. Dr. Sayel's consulting room door flew open and Nate stood framed in the doorway. "It's Orchid," I cried before he had a chance to say anything.

Dr. Sayel pushed past Nate to swiftly examine the baby. "She seems all right, just hungry. I can't leave Mrs. Murchin now. Nate, take the baby into my office. There's a baby bottle on the third shelf—"

"Got it," Nate said.

I trailed after Nate, wondering how Big Orchid could have done this to her baby. I'd been sure she'd have given her life for her child, but now she'd gone and left Baby Orchid, left her wrapped up in this dirty sheet, hungry and helpless.

How long had she been out there? "Thought I heard a howl sometime back, but I figured it was that Bolivar again," Nate was saying. He'd found the baby bottle and was now filling it with formula. "Sit down in the rocker," he directed me, "and let her at it."

There was the sound of voices from down the hall, and I could hear a woman shouting. Nate grinned. "Family Group's been lively tonight—Mrs. Santos's been opening up about her marriage." He paused. "You going to be okay? I've got to get back to the doc."

I nodded, he left, and I rocked away and watched Baby Orchid suck down nourishment. "How could your mother do this to you?" I muttered.

But then, the world was full of things for which there were no explanations. I thought about them until I heard the doctor's step outside and she came in, moving so quickly, there seemed to be a jet stream in her wake.

She scooped Baby Orchid, bottle and all, out of my arms and carried her to the consulting room across the hall to check her out. "Apart from being wet and scared and hungry, she's fine as far as I can tell," she told me. "Tell me again what happened to her. No, I don't mean how and where you found her—I want to know about the Jade Palace."

When I'd finished, Dr. Sayel was silent for a second. "They moved the illegal workers out of the restaurant late this afternoon. Big Orchid must have brought her baby here before that."

"But wouldn't somebody have seen her leave the baby? Heard the baby crying?"

"The baby must have been asleep. Besides, Big Orchid would have been careful to avoid people—that's why she hid her child in those bushes instead of bringing her up onto the porch." A frown creased Dr.

Sayel's forehead as she added, "It took a lot of courage for that woman to do what she did."

I stared at her in disbelief. "I can't believe you said that. No decent mother would leave her own baby!"

"Is that what you think?" Dr. Sayel asked.

"Yes, I do. I'd rather die. I would! I'd starve, I'd steal, I'd—I'd do anything before I abandoned my baby."

"She couldn't help it, Mai," Dr. Sayel said gently. "Look at it from her point of view. We at the center were kind to her; we helped her baby. This was probably the only safe place Big Orchid could think of."

Cooing to the baby, Dr. Sayel changed her diaper and wrapped her in a clean blanket. The room had become very quiet. I could hear Baby Orchid sucking away, and Nate's voice down the hall talking with a waiting patient, and Mrs. Santos yelling in Judy's office.

"If you think of it," Dr. Sayel said at last, "Big Orchid didn't have many options. She wanted a better life for her child—better than either the hell she lived in or the hardship she'd have to go back to."

"How could it be better when this baby will never even know what her mother looked like?" I shouted. Baby Orchid tensed, her tiny arms and legs spasming in fright at the loudness of my voice, but then started to suck on the bottle again. "It's *not* better," I repeated, and then I started to cry.

Dr. Sayel came over to me and put her arms around me and held me. She didn't say anything, and she didn't have to. Both of us knew I wasn't talking about the Orchids.

"She shouldn't have died," I sobbed against the doctor's shoulder. "It's not fair."

"No."

"Even if she lived, sh-she wouldn't have kept me. The way it happened—the last thing she'd want was to be pregnant by him—she must have hated me, too."

179

"There aren't any easy answers," Dr. Sayel said. She patted my back sympathetically but firmly. "Maybe there aren't any answers."

Which was great—just great. I drew away from the doctor, thinking, okay, Mai, you came all this way just to learn that there aren't any answers.

And really, what had I learned? Coming to Boston had been like going fishing, and instead of fish, snaring old boots and mud and debris. I'd dragged the truth about Mai Hongvan from Lien, but it still wasn't enough to tell me the thing I most needed to know.

As Lien would say, that was life. I wiped away my useless tears. Baby Orchid let go of the nipple and gave a hiccup of content. Dr. Sayel hefted her to her shoulder and patted her back much as she'd patted mine. "What's going to happen to her?" I asked.

"It depends. It's almost certain her mother's in this country illegally—which would make this baby an illegal immigrant, too. But if this child were born in this country, that would make her a citizen."

Dr. Sayel looked thoughtful. "I'll have to phone the police, and Judy will be in touch with a friend of hers who works at the Department of Social Services. Try not to worry, Mai. We'll do our darnedest to get this baby into a really good foster home."

Which meant, I thought sorrowfully, that Baby Orchid would grow up with a lot of questions, too. Questions for which there could be no answers.

I never did go back to the Spring Restaurant that night. I called my folks from the center, and they came over and got me. They spent some time talking with Dr. Sayel, so we were there when the police arrived. After several calls to DSS people about the availability of foster homes—which came up to exactly zero—it was agreed that Judy keep Baby Orchid overnight.

"And we'll see what tomorrow brings," the doctor told me when we said good-bye, but that didn't comfort me. For the Orchids, "tomorrow" hadn't exactly had a good track record.

The Houston clan was pretty silent as we headed back to the hotel, and Mom said if I needed to talk, she was there. I said I needed to think things through on my own.

"I understand," Mom said. Then she added, "Tomorrow's our last day in Boston. What do you say to cutting loose and seeing the sights like they've never been seen before?"

Sight-seeing has never been my thing, especially now, but I couldn't say no since both David and Liz were nuts about the idea. The senior Delaneys were working, but Shauna and those twins came with us.

It was quite a day. Mom and Dad were, like, complete tourists and lost in a world of their own. Shauna and Liz teamed up and totally ignored their younger brothers, so I ended up having to constantly chase the boys down and threaten to lock them up in the car if they didn't quit acting like gerbils.

In a way, this was good. I was so busy that I didn't have time to think of anything else. Later, after we'd dropped the Delaney kids off and were riding a taxi back to the hotel, Mom said, "Such dear children. I'm sorry that Jon couldn't make it today, though."

"So is Mai," Liz giggled, and the brat turned around to aim the ray gun he'd bought at Quincy Market Hall toward me.

"Mai's in love with Jo-on," he chanted. "Mai's in looove."

Mercifully, we'd by now reached our hotel. I marched in, determined to lose my little brother before I did him serious bodily harm, but stopped when I heard my name being called. When I turned my head, I saw Lien sitting in one of the lobby chairs.

Of all the people I *didn't* want to see just then— but I couldn't ignore her. Mom and Dad were already walking over to her, and Liz jiggled my good arm and breathed, "Is she really as mean as she looks?"

Lien looked as she always did, frizzed hair, rimless

181

glasses, bright pink blouse tucked into dark pants. She didn't look especially mean—but then, I'd gotten used to her unsmiling, stern expression.

"Mai," Mom called, "Lien wants to talk to you."

About what? I wondered. She'd told me about Mai Hongvan, and about the lowlife who had fathered me. Nancy had told me yesterday how she felt about me. All in all, what else was left to say?

Unwillingly, I walked over to where Lien sat, and she said, "Tomorrow, you leave." I nodded. "I don't come to airport," she went on. "We are very busy at restaurant now, so others can't come either."

In a way, I was relieved, except that I'd have liked to have seen Vinny again. I told her, that was fine, and she related how busy the restaurant had been since the Jade Palace closed. "And Pearls don't bother us no more, either—they too worried about police watching them."

My folks said they had packing to do, shook hands good-bye, and left, taking Liz and David with them. "Mrs. Houston say, if Vinh like, he can come stay with you in Iowa next summer," Lien said. "You like that?"

"It'd be great," I cried, really meaning it, and then we were both quiet, thinking of Vinny and the Pearls and poor Tommy Vuong.

"Maybe I send him to Iowa, then. Maybe I send to my cousin, who live in San Diego. Anyway, I will get Vinh out of Brighton next summer—but right now he doing okay with Mr. Singh."

Lien's narrow eyes glittered as she recounted that Mr. Singh was now talking of hiring Vinny permanently. "He work at Megabytes in afternoon. Work at restaurant during rush time. Rest of time, he study. Everybody satisfy."

Lien looked triumphant. She'd never change, I figured. Even now she was still telling Vinny what to do.

But at least she was trying to see it his way. "How is Nancy?" I ventured to ask.

Lien cut me a glance that said, you ought to know. "I try talk with her—she don't want to speak with me. Last night at restaurant I ask Mrs. Houston, what to do. She say, leave door open, try to communicate. Nice woman, Mrs. Houston—"

She broke off and pulled a piece of paper from her purse. "Here," she said. "Grandma Bach Thi's recipe for spring roll. Make for sure you don't let nobody outside family into secret."

Touched, I thanked her. She nodded and then said abruptly, "This is for you, too."

Surprised, I took the tissue-wrapped object from her and, opening it, looked down at a small, plastic-backed hand mirror. "This belonged to my sister, Mai," Lien informed me. "It is only thing of hers I keep. Now it is yours."

My hand shook. In my hand, my face in the mirror looked blankly back at me. "Uh, thank you," I heard myself say.

Lien chewed her thin lower lip and then said in her short, peppery way, "War make people change, ha? People like old man Vuong. Like Diep. They don't understand that world they knew has gone forever, so inside they grow sad and weak. I change, too. Grow too strong, maybe. Only my sister Mai does not change."

The hotel lobby and everyone in it seemed to slide away until there was only Lien and myself in the world. "When you were born, she was happy," Lien went on. "She held you in her arms, say you are so beautiful. Two days later, she die. Before she die, she ask me to take care of you."

My throat hurt to ask the question. "Then she didn't want to—to give me away?"

"*She* never give. But she ask *me*, do best for you, ha? So I think, what is best for you? You are both Vietnamese and American, and your Vietnamese mother, she is dead. I do not know if we will ever leave refugee camp, how we will live." Lien paused to draw breath and then went on. "Nguyen is sick.

You are so small. I don't want you die, like Khi, so I think it is best for you to be adopt in some kind American family that can give you everything."

She held out her hands palm upward, and in that small gesture I saw the Tranhs' desperate life in the refugee camp. Then I thought of Mom and Dad and my brother and sister and our house in Serena. My family and all it had meant to me.

Lien leaned forward to tap the mirror in my hand. "You don't look like my sister, but that's not important. Ha? Once, this was my sister's mirror, but now it yours. When you look it, you must see your own face."

She paused, struggling with words to try to express what she meant. "Past all finished. Present don't stay for long. Future coming, and no one can stop it. That future belongs to you."

She reached out and, in the first gesture of affection she'd ever shown me, cupped my cheek in the palm of her hard, dry hand. Then, before I could react, she'd gotten up and stalked out of the hotel.

So I sat alone in the hotel lobby and looked down into the mirror in my hand. My face looked back at me. Unchanged, the same as always: dark, straight fall of hair, hazel-brown eyes, straight nose, not-quite-olive skin. The face that Jon had seen so clearly from the first, the face that didn't really reflect Mai Hongvan or the Houstons, much as I loved them.

My face.

But who are you? whispered the ghost of that old, taunting, familiar voice in my mind. *Who might you be, Mai?*

And I answered: I am Mai Jennifer Houston, born of Mai Hongvan, child of Vivian and Leo Houston, sister to Liz and David, citizen of the United States, member of the world, and a small but important part of the universe.

"*That's* who I am, okay?" I whispered, and the face

in my mirror suddenly smiled at me through my tears.

As Lien had warned, none of the Tranhs came to see me off at Logan Airport. Mom was a little surprised and Dad rumbled that it was shoddy manners, but I was cool with it.

"Cool, schmool," Dad snorted. He hated to fly and had worked himself into a royal state of nerves and bad temper. "I'd have thought that at least Diep Tranh would have come to see Mai off."

He addressed this to Mom, but she was too busy yelling at David, who was ducking behind chairs in the terminal and shooting his disgusting gun. It didn't help that Logan was a mob scene. Kids were coming home or going away on last-minute vacations. Tourists were lining up to try to get on overbooked flights as standbys.

Meanwhile my dad was checking tickets for the millionth time. Liz had ambled over to the newsstand and was looking through a magazine as if she didn't know any of us, and Mom looked so frazzled that I went and bought her a cup of coffee.

"Enjoy it," I said automatically as she lifted the container to her lips.

"Believe me, I will. I needed this!" Mom sighed as she added, "Baby, I'll be glad when we get home. Big cities are fine, but—*David*, will you quit that, please?—good grief, where has that boy gotten to now?"

Just then my name was called and Jon came running over toward us. Hard on his heels strode Dr. Sayel, and farther down the way trotted Judy, holding a baby in her arms.

"We made it," Jon said as he scooped me up in a bone-bruising bear hug. "I'm here representing the clan. Mom had to work at the last minute, Shauna has an overnight at her camp, and the twins are sick, so Dad had to stay home and take care of them. They all sent their love."

185

"And we wanted to wish you bon voyage, so we picked Jon up at Luigi's and brought him along," Dr. Sayel added briskly. She patted my cheek and shook hands with my folks while Judy puffed up to us.

"Wanted to tell you it looks like Baby Orchid's all set," she panted. "We've got a super foster family lined up. Don't worry, I'll keep tabs on her. Promise. Look, she's smiling at you."

Dr. Sayel's magic was working on Dad—he almost looked calm. Mom was rounding up David and Liz. "Can I hold her?" I asked Judy.

She put the baby into my arms, and I wondered at the change in her as she chortled up at me. Wide-awake, impish, pink-cheeked, and bright-eyed, and so cute you could eat her with a spoon. "Hey, Orchid," I whispered.

She chuckled at me again, shifting in my arms, and I felt a tug of both happiness and sorrow. Mom had held me like this. So had Mai Hongvan. And now I knew that they had both held me with love.

"Listen," my dad was rumbling, "we're boarding the plane right now. Did you hear me, you kids? Vivian, where are my tickets?"

Mom put a hand on his arm. "Leo, they're only preboarding," she soothed. "We have *time*."

Baby Orchid would grow up with her own questions. There were a lot of those around for sure, but at least I'd learned one answer. I pressed my cheek against the baby's and whispered that hard-won secret in her tiny ear.

"The only person you have to be is yourself," I told her. "Don't be afraid to be everything that you want to be."

Then I gave her back to Judy, hugged her, hugged Dr. Sayel, and right in front of my family gave Jon a big kiss.

"Thanks," I told him, "for being there for me. For seeing *me*."

And then I followed my family into the big silver bird that would take us all home.